The
Witch Market

The Witch Market
Copyright 2014 by Catherine Geiger

Images Copyright 2014 by Claudia Caranfa (Kittrose)
kittrose.blogspot.com

This is a work of fiction. All people and places depicted in this book are of the author's imagination, and any resemblance to real people or places is purely coincidental. Except for the Xs, they are absolutely real.

Published by Piscataqua Press
An imprint of RiverRun Bookstore, Inc.
142 Fleet St., Portsmouth, NH. 03801

www.riverrunbookstore.com
www.piscataquapress.com

ISBN: 978-1-939739-31-5

Printed in the United States of America

PISCATAQUA
PRESS

The
Witch Market

By Catherine Geiger

ONE

Outside the Witch Market, there are no sirens. There are no sirens, so there is no warning of the Xs' arrival.

The first to go is a child.

He is playing in the dirt, drawing misshapen Sanskrit letters that his mother showed him only yesterday. His face is bright, splotched with grime, but his skin is still baby-soft and tender. His thatch of darkish hair sticks up near the back, where he's been twirling strands with sticky fingers. He sits outside the family tent constructed of layers of tarps and poles, in which he lives with his mother, father, grandmother, and three siblings. This tent is up near the scant light. There are not many near it. A soft orange glow shines through the thin walls of the tent. A few early morning figures move slowly within it.

The crunch of boots on gravel makes the child look up from his juvenile lettering. His eyes are large and dark. His left thumb is in his mouth. He is four years old.

An X stands a few yards away. The unnatural yellow jumpsuit conceals gender. The X raises its weapon. It speaks, the question phrased as a statement.

"What's your favorite color?"

Then the X presses the small orange button on the underside of the weapon.

In a few milliseconds, the tiny bullet has entered the child's forehead, mashing the frontal lobes. It travels down the neck, busting the heart, puncturing both lungs, and then travels back up the neck and exits the body at the top of the spinal cord.

The bullet falls into the dirt.

The child is already dead.

The child was dead ever since the X pushed the orange button.

Ever since he looked up from his messy Sanskrit.

There are no sirens, so there is no warning of the Xs' arrival.

There are no sirens, so everyone outside the Witch Market is dead.

The grandmother is second.

"Quillan! Quillan, get up!"

Quillan Bratumil Oddanie opens his eyes. They are usually bleary when he wakes. Six a.m. is no different. It's early. Dark out still. But it's often dark down here.

"Quillan!"

He knows that tone.

He's heard it only once before.

Immediately, all the bleariness is gone. Grainne stands over him, her reddish hair in a knot. She's terrified. Quillan can hear them. The Xs. Not in the distance. They are close. He can hear their boots, the screams, the shrieking. He can hear the swift, fleshy noise the bullet makes as it penetrates an unsuspecting forehead.

Grainne hugs him to her. The thin blankets of Quillan's cot are caught between their bodies.

"Mum—" he whispers.

"I love you," she breathes in his ear.

His heart is beating quicker and quicker.

"Where are the Ks?" he says.

"Daddy's getting the girls."

Indeed, he hears them too, rustling on the other side of the plastic tarp.

"I love you."

"I love you, Mum."

"Go."

"The girls—"

"Right behind you. Go."

"What about you?"

"Right behind you."

"I love you."

"I love you, Quillan."

"Right behind me?"

"Go."

She kisses him and slowly lifts the back flap of the tent. She's shaking. The Ks slip through a slit in the adjoining tarp. Klaudia and Kassia. Their eyes are massive blue saucers. Bialas follows. Kassia moves to the side, clings to her father's leg. Grainne holds the back flap a little higher.

"Go, Quillan."

He gets down, slips beneath the flap feet first, trying not to crinkle it. He's almost out of the tent. Kassia exhales, a deep, shuddering breath.

First is the swift sound, cutting through the tent. Then the fleshy end, as the bullet burrows into Klaudia's head and exits. Kassia screams. A larger bullet tears into Bialas' leg, the one shielding his daughter. Another swift-fleshy sound. Quillan registers it only after Grainne crumples.

Go, Quillan.

He grabs Kassia and bolts. Bialas runs after them, limping, fighting to stay upright.

A leg. A leg saved Kassia.

Klaudia was lame.

A leg killed her.

Kassia is crying. She can see over his shoulder. Not good. Quillan tucks her lower, holds her face against his neck. The tears gush down his shirt.

Keep running, Dad. Keep running, dammit.

Quillan's heart is running a marathon. Inhale exhale inhale exhale.

Breathe.

Grainne.

Oh God, Mum. Oh God.

Quillan runs. He navigates tents, huts, scrap houses, tents, heaps, fences. He runs. He doesn't look back. *Right behind me.*

Around him are others. People. Screaming. Running. Breathing. Falling. Snitches. *Snitches.*

Snitches and Xs.

He can hear everything. Every boot, every breath, every swift-fleshy noise. He hears the larger bullets. They make deep, loud popping sounds. *PoPddpoPdd.* Kassia's tears surge down his chest. She's shaking, clinging, sobbing, struggling to breathe. Klaudia. Grainne.

Oh God, Mum.

Quillan clutches her tighter.

"It's gonna be okay, it's gonna be okay, Daddy's okay, Daddy's alive, Kassia, Daddy's okay—"

Run, Dad. Run.

Too soon, Quillan trips and falls in the dark behind a sheet of metal. Kassia screams. He can hear them. The Xs. Coming closer.

Funny how they never run. As though they have all the time in the world.

Another swift-fleshy. Nearby, a man crumples. His hair is not white.

Quillan lies dazed on the ground.

Keep running, Dad.

Kassia shakes her brother.

"Quillan," she whimpers, "Quillan-"

He raises his head. Catches her dripping face in his hands. Holds it steady.

"Breathe, Kassi."

She's shaking. She's terrified. Poor Kassia.

"Breathe, Kassi. Breathe. Can you do that for me?"

She nods, shuddering, but breathing.

"Good girl. I love you, Kassia."

"I love you, Quillan."

"I know you do. Breathe. See the fence lines?"

He gently guides her head so that she's looking in the direction he was running. There are rows of chain link and mesh fencing not far away, riddled with holes and slits.

"I want you to run."

"Quillan—"

"Run, Kassia. Breathe. Breathe."

She takes a few more tremulous breaths.

"Good girl. Run. Stay low. Don't look back."

She runs.

He watches. Listens. There are more swift-fleshies. More deep-pops. None too near though. A tent catches fire and light flies everywhere, like an army of fireflies released from a jar. Oranges and yellows that bite and claw at the gritty ground. He counts down from five and runs.

A leg killed Klaudia.

A leg saved Kassia.

Keep running, Dad.

Breathe, Kassi.

Oh God, Mum. Oh God.

Quillan runs to the fence line, scrabbles over the top of a chain link, the holes too small for him to fit through. Another chain link. Another. Now the mesh. The mesh is too tall and flimsy to climb over, but the hard plastic is torn in spots and he finds places to fit through. Around him, people escape the Xs. The south door is near. And others will have their own secret ways into the Witch Market.

A woman with curly hair wiggles beneath the last of the mesh fencing that Quillan is trying to force himself through. The escape she used is too tight for him. Cleophas would be able to fit through it. *Where is Cleophas?*

The woman's curly hair screams another name at him.

Quillan freezes.

Lord.

Dana.

Quillan tears at the mesh, trying to loosen the horrible, unyielding fibers. There are sharp wires embedded in the plastic. He tears at the slit in the mesh until his hands are raw and scraped from loops of naked wire. He can hear the Xs approaching. His heart thumps a hurricane.

The mesh weakens enough and Quillan squeezes one arm through, one leg, head, shoulders, other leg. His left arm is stuck. His hand is caught. Tangled in a mess of naked wires and toothy plastic mesh.

Breathe.

There are more deep-pops now. *PoPddpoPdd.* The occasional swift-fleshy.

A man stops beside Quillan, a man he knows. Not Bialas. This man has brown hair, not white. Tancred takes Quillan's hand, tries to force it through the mesh, but the wires are biting into his skin, eating his wrist and fingers.

Tancred grabs Quillan's shoulder.

"Bite the fence!" he orders.

Quillan looks at him wildly, but as Tancred seizes his hand, he conforms, biting the edge of the mesh. With a sickening, twisting movement, Tancred breaks Quillan's hand. Pain races up his arm and his teeth sink into the mesh. Blinking back tears, he helps Tancred wiggle his broken hand from the wires, but his pinky finger only jerks. The wires have cut too deep into his flesh. Try as he may, Quillan cannot get free.

Breathe.

The ground crunches beneath the boots of the Xs, the chain link fences melting before them. They crumple red-hot and burning on the grit.

Tancred has seized Quillan's hand again, pressing it against what is left of the mesh. He takes a short object from his pocket. The little blade winks and suddenly fire eats up Quillan's veins, burning and frying his nerves, stabbing them with little pins of ice and acid, and he screams, almost animal-like, as the fire of pain consumes his hand. He does not realize when the latter half of his pinky finger has been severed. For a moment, the pain cancels out sound. Then he hears the swift-fleshy noise and sees Tancred fall through the mesh.

Other hands grab him and pull him towards a great titanium sheet set in the ground. There is a small crevice in it, through which the last Snitches rush. Quillan is thrust through onto an incline, and before he sees it, he hears it. The south door is open, wide open, like a mammoth mouth. It's closing.

Quillan is thrown inside, thrown through the south door into the Witch Market, carried along with the current of Snitches. The fire is eating his hand, his stump of a finger. The south door is still closing.

"Quillan!"

The voice is shrill, desperate, relieved, jubilant, horrified. A young woman forces her way through the crowd, her crutch knocked aside by the current.

Dana.

But all Quillan is seeing is Tancred. Tancred falling through the mesh. Tancred's body dropping onto his own. Swift-fleshy.

His eyes blow up and he pivots to the door.

"Stop it! Stop it, Quillan!" Dana shouts, grabbing his shirt and dragging him back as he struggles against her.

"I have to get Tancred!" Quillan cries frantically, "I have to get him, Dana! I have to get his body!"

He's sobbing, shouting, blood streaming from his broken hand and sad, butchered finger.

"No, Quillan! Quillan, *STOP IT, NO, HE'S DEAD!*"

Dana screams as Quillan wrenches from her grip. She picks up a piece of heavy metal pipe and throws it at him. Its jagged edge strikes his calves and he topples to the ground with a gasp. He strains to regain his feet, and ends up crawling to the great metal door. But the south door has closed, its teeth sunken into the metal surrounding it. Quillan crawls to where the dirt and metal meet and at the south door he rises to his knees and slams his arms against the thing. He hammers on it, yelling, sobbing, cursing. The metal makes tinny sounds as he beats it. The fire laces his injured hand. Blood stains the door.

When Dana reaches him, hobbling-jerking-crawling on her bad leg, Quillan still hits the door, but he is defeated. He thumps the metal with agonizing chokes, emotion caught in his throat. Dana rescues his hand from another blow and he slumps to the ground and entangles himself in her limbs, shaking, grimy tears dripping from his nose and chin. Dana nails her arms about him, his bloody, broken, swollen hand cupped between their heaving bodies.

"I'm sorry," she says, her eyes watering as the two of them shake, tremors ripping through one body to the other and back.

"He saved me — he saved me, Dana — the Xs —"

"They'll burn him —"

"His body."

"It's gone."

Five dirty tears drip into the curly labyrinth of Dana's hair. Blood soaks their clothing, hot. The roiling activity of the Witch Market screams in Quillan's ears.

"Dana, is Kassia—?"

"She's here. I saw her."

"Is my dad?"

"I don't know, Quillan."

Quillan quakes, curling up in her grasp. Dana's eyes squeeze shut, her palms pressing tightly to his back, gripping him as though someone will appear beside them and try to rip him away.

"Dana, the Xs—they got—they got Klaudia—"

"Oh, Quillan."

"They—they got my mum—"

She holds him closer, grips his body tighter, so tight that it is almost painful, burrowing her head against his neck. His calves are throbbing from the pipe she threw after him.

"I'm so sorry."

"I'm sorry."

Her nailed arms clutch him and cover his ears, and he shakes and rocks and holds her to him—left hand between their bellies, right hand cemented about her waist—weeping, shuddering with grief and pain.

TWO

At three forty-one a.m., May sixth, 2090, the fifty-millionth citizen of Boston, Massachusetts is born. Female; seven pounds, four ounces. Her name is Lana. Her birth is documented, and at three forty-one a.m. and forty seconds, Boston becomes BostonMaxia. With fifty million official citizens, BostonMaxia joins the other population giants of the United States; NYCMax, LosAngelesMax, SanFranMax, ChicagoMaxia, HoustonMaxia, PheonixMax and PhiDelMax, to name a few.

At three forty-two a.m., the Boxians begin to celebrate.

"Lana" rockets to crown the most popular baby name polls for both girls and boys. Intricate fireworks are set off, depicting the newborn's face, name, and birth details, as well as the new population figures. Cosmetics are made to fit the infant's skin type, estimated eye color. Thirty new fragrances are advertised in her honor. A special beverage is mixed and launched with her name. "Luminescent Limelight" is deemed the color of the occasion, a hue the perfect dazzling blend of effervescent green, metallic yellow and silvery off-white.

In the Cassiopeia, the city's newest and most luxurious penthouse, a party is underway. Thousands of Boxians, both residents of and guests to the penthouse, walk on the many floors, discussing the choice of their extravagant evening wear, and suggesting to their conversational partners that they try the pineapple and fennel crab cake, as the combination of flavors is just too sublimely attractive. Of course, the newest citizen of BostonMaxia is the ripest bit of talk, but only so much can be said about an infant not even twenty-four hours old, so the conversations quickly transmute to every kind of possible matter pertaining to expensive impracticality.

Many of the partygoers gather at the large windows to observe the fireworks, gasping at those they find mesmeric, and when deemed the appropriate reaction to loud explosions, giving a small excited start. Some Boxians abandon the windows and instead cluster along the wide sparkling walks that stretch between the pinnacles of the Cassiopeia, standing in the open air to watch the fireworks burst against the ceiling of smog that floats above the city. The fireworks eventually give way to a more complex laser show, and the many colored lights turn the Cassiopeia from its usual silver and white state to a work of ruby, sapphire, clementine and ultramarine.

The Cassiopeia is one of the city's most intriguing constructions. Built on the outer edge of the city, where the floods of air traffic zoom in from the nearest maxias, NYCMax and PhiDelMax, it shows off the radiance of the city. It is similarly shaped to an hourglass or a tree, with a wide base and slender middle. Above the architectural abdomen, the penthouse widens again and splits into three pinnacles, the middle tower being the stoutest of the trio, the other two built at outwards diagonal angles. This abstract letter W that is the top of the penthouse, as well as the building's name, is a tribute to the Cassiopeia constellation, which was long ago hidden with the rest of the stars by the smog. The architect behind the Cassiopeia has directed the construction of other constellational buildings across the United States. Each maxia has one of its own. The Cassiopeia is the newest of these creations. It was built in a month, once the due date of Miss Fifty-Millionth was secured.

Below one of the numerous viaducts branching between the three towers is a small black hoverbike, tucked away from the eyes of the flashing laser show and security sentries that prowl about the penthouse. The hoverbike is propped up on a tidy ledge in a corner where bridge and middle tower fuse. On the bike is a boyish young man in his late teens. His name is Cleophas Quana Ektos. He is what the Boxians call a Snitch.

Cleophas has a light complexion and pale, flaxen hair. He wears a crumpled black coat, several sizes too big for him. Coupled with his thin frame, it makes him look even smaller than he already is. His hands, wrapped in fallow-colored bandages stained with grime and grease, clutch the handles of the bike, but his eyes are trained on the walk above him. It curves away from the tower slightly, so that from his corner Cleophas can glimpse the Boxians as they make amiable talk and admire the laser show.

At five a.m., it is not uncommon for the Boxians to be up and about; the city never seems to sleep and is at all hours bustling with noise, lights and air traffic. For the Snitches, who live in the Witch Market beneath the city, there is little reason in being awake so early. But it is not unusual for Cleophas, who is often insomniac, to be active in the early hours of the morning. He's a curious, intuitive person, and likes to observe the Boxians, despite their strange hobbies and interests.

It is, however, foolish for him to be Up.

It is foolish for any of the Snitches to go Up.

"Snitch" is the name coined by the Boxians for any person who lives in what is referred to by the Snitches themselves as the Witch Market. The Boxians have no knowledge of the

Witch Market, which is an invaluably good thing. As far as the Boxians are concerned, Snitches are pests, the very lowest of the low.

The Snitches protect old art and magic, faiths and spiritual beliefs of a bygone age, making the Witch Market a melting pot of international cultures and civilizations. They are the librarians and curators of art and literature, preserving antique culture against the Culture Wipe.

It was the pinnacle of the Technological Revolution that induced the Culture Wipe. In 2030, when the first maxia, NYCMax, was constructed in New York City, a vote was held to discontinue funding and preservation of the old arts. The maxias would forge the way for a fresh, new culture; no longer would the country be lugging around the burden of departed ages. There would be new inventions, new literature, creations and ideas not carved from the old nation but constructed anew by the frontrunners of the country. The United States would be dazzling, the role model of the world.

Despite the Snitches' best attempts, there were not enough votes to overrun the Culture Wipe. As the new laws were set in place, the Snitches ran around procuring as much old culture as they could. Discrimination towards them grew immensely, until eventually the Snitches were forced underground, where they created the Witch Market and have remained ever since.

More than culture and art and literature, the Snitches also preserve magic. The place is a sanctuary for those who still believe in the old ways, the practices of the supernatural, and those who continue to bless the earth and its wondrous but depleting bounty.

None of the Snitches are truly magical; however, there are a few who have certain traits and abilities that are deemed so. These traits are rooted in the Snitches' beliefs. Some show signs of weak telekinetic ability, but can only control natural things, materials that come from the earth. A few have blurred foresight, while others carry faint characteristics of long gone mythical beings. The most commonly found attribute is that of heightened sensory perception; sight, hearing, touch, taste and smell.

But to the Boxians, who know next to nothing of the Snitches, these people are thought of as pests.

The Snitches go Up only when they are starving or freezing, and even then, only when they have no other options. Once there, they go dumpster diving for the food they cannot grow underground, stealing and scavenging for the supplies they cannot produce. Often, they steal from supply vans. The Boxians view such rummaging the same as that of any rat or roach. In their conversations, the word 'Snitch' is synonymous with 'pest', and pests are exterminated.

This revelation led to the conception of the Xs.

Every once in a while, the Xs are tipped off. They go to the given location, usually in a slummy, rundown part of Lower City, and exterminate. They kill, but do not pursue. Possibly they realize that like the rats and roaches, BostonMaxia cannot be rid of all the Snitches at once. They are more like machines than people, the Xs.

*   *   *

On the viaduct above Cleophas is a young woman. She is standing at the guardrail among a quartet of other guests, but rather than actively engaging in their trivial conversation, she quietly observes the laser show. She is tall, wearing a straight, long metallic dress in colors of deep shiny browns, gold, and black. The dress hugs her midsection and has a high, sleeveless top. When she turns slightly, Cleophas can see that the back of the dress slopes to just above her backside. Her skin is dark, the color of coffee, and not inked or dyed as far as can be seen, except for three thin, horizontal, satiny olive green lines below each of her eyes. Her eyes, unlike her skin, are not their natural hue; the irises are a thick, buttery yellow, but that is the only alteration, for the pupils and whites are untouched. Her hair is thin and short, cut along her jawbone, a little higher in the back. It is dark red, parted down the middle of her scalp. Her lips are naked, as are her wrists and neck, but her eyelids and fingernails are painted bronze, and a single band is on her right middle finger, the same shade of green as the tattoos beneath her eyes.

Reservedly watching the laser show, hands serenely clasped on the guardrail, she can easily be any age between eighteen and twenty-five.

Cleophas has never seen her before, which is not in the least surprising, given the fifty million official citizens of BostonMaxia. She fascinates him. Her appearance, though outlandish from one point of view, is quite tame when compared with that of her fellows; one is swathed in a glowing, sea foam-colored, bubble-like article that can hardly be called clothing, while another companion is wearing what looks like a faceted, ruby-red beehive atop his head. This woman with the butter-colored eyes is different, Cleophas feels. She's attractive, almost beautiful, but that is not quite what it is. She seems —

displaced?

For some reason, Cleophas can't imagine her in the setting of the typical, high-ranking Boxian citizen; at ease to lounge about her luxurious residence, accepting and sending party invitations, consuming fine food, constantly being shuffled about to different fittings for countless flashy occasions. She seems genuinely interested in the laser show, but could she be interested in something more? Like old literature, or arithmetic, or stars? Cleophas wonders if this woman knows what the stars look like, if she can hear them. Then he shakes his head.

No. Only Blathnat can hear the stars.

But Blathnat doesn't smell like this woman.

This woman smells like fresh roses, the large, peach-colored kind with thick petals. Layered over the aroma of roses is a warm, husky, oaky scent; woody, rich and good. Peachy roses and oak. Cleophas tilts his head back a fraction, closing his eyes. He inhales and his narrow nostrils flare, lolling in the lavishness of the scent. A soft breath slips from between his thin lips. Many of the perfumes worn by the Boxians are overwhelming concoctions, put together with bizarrely ill taste, yet they buy the petite jewel-toned bottles with ridiculous names and equally ridiculous prices with no thought at all, except to join or begin the newest fetish.

This woman, however, has fine taste. She has picked a gorgeous scent, one of the most enchanting smells Cleophas's nose has ever detected. Surely she must know that she has done right by her choice, that she has not fallen prey to the traps of the marketers and cheap perfumers, and has instead chosen a ripe, beautiful scent unhindered by thickness and heavy additions. Surely she recognizes the beauty of the product she wears.

She must.

The Boxians are not bad people, Cleophas thinks,

swallowing another waft of the peachy rose, oaky scent. Gulping it down.

Foolish sometimes. But not bad.

Does that mean the Xs are not bad people?

Another draft of perfume. This young woman, she's special. She's different. She's not like the rest of the Boxians, who behave like silly birds, flouncing about from one roost to another, showing off their feathers. She's more like a tree. A slender tree, waving in the wind, relaxed... loose.

She'd smile if she were a tree.

More of the peachyrose/oaky smell floods his olfactory senses. He gulps it down. Inhales the roses. Gulps the oak.

But she's more like a willow than an oak.

Without that straight, metallic dress, she probably has curves. Small curves, but curves all the same. And she's tall. Of course, the dress is floor-length, hiding the height of her shoes, but even without the anonymous shoes, she's probably still tall.

Willowy.

And with that red hair —

like a willow in autumn.

But, Cleophas realizes, he doesn't know if willows turn red in autumn. Maybe they're orange. Or even brown.

Blathnat might know.

At six a.m., the laser show ends and the young woman with the butter-colored eyes leaves the viaduct. Cleophas stretches his bandaged fingers and sighs softly. He will likely never see her again, never again come across those butter-colored eyes, whose owner has such impeccably fine taste in scent.

A quarter of an hour later, after observing a few more Boxians cross the viaduct, Cleophas decides to leave. He needs to allow himself plenty of time to guarantee a chance at a safe return to the Witch Market. It's nearly dawn though. Dawn isn't good. The dark is a better friend to the Snitches.

Cleophas has been naïve.

He's been Up too long.

Cleophas

THREE

Cleophas waits for the nearest Boxians to leave the viaduct as he puts on his helmet. He counts down from thirty, his fingers tensing on the handles of the hoverbike, and then puts the bike into gear. The engine purrs softly. He will have one chance to make it down the Cassiopeia. The moment he drops from the ledge, he will have left this fragment of safe space and be open game for any security guard that spies him. Cleophas closes his eyes, murmurs a prayer, and revs the hoverbike off the ledge.

Free falling doesn't even set in; the bike zooms down the side of the Cassiopeia's shortest pinnacle, stealthily avoiding lights, alarms, windows, walks, and balconies by sticking to the shadows. The hoverbike does not make much noise, which is fortunate; it zips down, completely vertical, a hair's breadth between the Cassiopeia's glossy siding and the bike's slick underside.

The majority of the air traffic begins at about where the three pinnacles split from the building's midsection. In one quick motion, Cleophas pulls the hoverbike up from its dive to leave the Cassiopeia behind and plunge through the multitude of traffic, weaving along intricate lines of patterns only he can recognize. It is all about timing and quick thinking when it comes to cutting through the airways; knowing which lanes are dominated by the massive Greyhound shuttles, which ones frequented by fast food delivery pods. The florescent orange and yellow taxis always screaming at the speed regulations are the worst. Cleophas has developed a system for himself when it comes to navigating these busiest airways of the city, built up from years of observation and close calls. It is incredibly dangerous, he knows, and the odds are rarely in his favor, but Cleophas never takes such a life-endangering risk without taking great caution along as well. Patience is a precious virtue, one Cleophas is lucky enough to have been blessed with, particularly being a Snitch, but sometimes speed equals invisibility in the world of BostonMaxia, for what citizen would later remember seeing a black hoverbike splitting through heavy air traffic outside the Cassiopeia?

Once out of the zoo of traffic, Cleophas halts the bike for a moment on an empty rooftop, far below the Cassiopeia. The ride through the lanes, though less than a minute long, is always terrifying, and he allows himself a moment to catch his breath, thrilled to be intact.

Nonetheless, he's trembling and sweating under his huge coat, and the horizon is starting to glow softly.

Cleophas starts the bike again and it lifts off from the rooftop a fraction. He slowly maneuvers the hoverbike to the edge of the roof and then revs it into another dive, deep into the maze that is Lower City.

Lower City and Upper City form the two different zones of BostonMaxia, unofficially dubbed as such by the citizens. Upper City is where buildings like the Cassiopeia dwell and where high society lives. It is the glitzy, flashy, flamboyant face of the city, the place that attracts tourists and VIPs like ants to sugar. Everything in Upper City is bright, shiny and new. Not a thing there is more than sixty years old. Anything older than that is in Lower City.

While Upper City is built up from the roofs of Lower City, Lower City is built up from the foundations of old Boston. There are some nice parts of Lower City, there's no doubt about it. However, there are many places in Lower City that are particularly old and rundown, undesirable to cross at any hour of day or night. Lower City is the home of the middle class, the working class, and the slum-dwellers. Affable, hardworking folk living alongside homeless bums, all steering clear of the repulsive crowd of thieves, drug dealers, rapists, and pimps.

But even the druggies and prostitutes have standings. The slimmest standings of all, it can be certain, but at least they have that, because no one is below the Snitches.

The ride through Lower City will be the longest part of Cleophas's trip back to the Witch Market, but it will be much safer. There are not enough police in Lower City to patrol every district equally and they are usually more concentrated in the areas of heavier crime. The black hoverbike will be subtle; nonetheless, he knows to watch his speed in the more populated zones. It will be the worst thing if Cleophas is pulled over; his lack of an ID will paradoxically identify him either as a cipher or a Snitch and there are no good outcomes for either. At least being a Snitch, his death would be one of quick insignificance.

In time Cleophas enters an exceedingly rundown part of Lower City. There are still Boxians about, but they quickly become few and far between as the hoverbike zips through a complex work of crumbling streets and what is left of the habitable residences gives away. Soon there are no people at all, not even vagabonds. No one lives down here, deep in the dark, in the remnants of old Boston. There are just desolate shells of buildings and roads, untouched for decades and left to putrefy in the shadows that lurk at the bottom of the city.

Alone, zipping by in a rush of quiet sound, Cleophas is

pacified. There is a quietness down here that is unequaled anywhere else in BostonMaxia; a silence very heavy, very old, very real. Zooming past on the hoverbike, black coat billowing like a parachute, Cleophas is swallowed. The exoskeletons of the buildings, pitted and dark, are spitted with titanic abutments of transparent alumina, looking ghostly in their transparency. The tiny bits of light that fit through the chinks in the ceiling high, high above quickly disappear in the darkness, but where the alumina thrusts into the roots of Lower City the light glitters, trapped, turning the alumina to softly sparkling towers of crystal.

The place is reminiscent of a Gothic cathedral, and Cleophas is reverent and respectful, flying down the aisles of cracked pavement between the pews of decrepit shops and forgotten businesses.

When an overpass emerges from the gloom, gray and deteriorating, Cleophas slows the hoverbike. The overpass marks the beginning of one of two areas where Snitches can be found living outside the Witch Market. The other is near a slummy part of Lower City, with Boxians living not far away. Not many Snitches live there due to the insecurity the light brings; more live here, in the dark about the overpass. A scattering of dwellings between the two more concentrated areas links both locations.

Cleophas lives behind the overpass with his family, near to his cousin and best friend, Quillan. Quillan will tell him off for going Up, but his underlying curiosity will eventually get him to ask about what Cleophas has seen, and he will listen intently. Another good friend, Dana, will read him the riot act once she gets wind that he went Up again and he will cringe as she launches her tirade.

Cleophas's thin lips spread in a smile.

Suddenly, the smile falters. His bandaged hands tense on the handles of the hoverbike. A flower of insecurity blooms in his stomach, cringing and frightened and the bit of warmth he feels evaporates.

There is light at the overpass. Not the soft glows that usually spot the Snitches' tents, but harsh, hungry light that jumps up and down with tall tongues.

Yellow jumpsuits move among the flames.

Panic sets a different fire to Cleophas. He cuts a hard right with the hoverbike and turns off the headlight, pulling up behind a lopsided bakery. His heart booms within his chest. Acrid smoke curls in his nostrils, drifting over from the overpass. Blood, carnage and ruin flood his senses.

The Xs. How did the Xs find them? When did they get here? How many are dead?

Quillan.

Quillan and Mum and Dad and Helminette.
Gamma Lucy and Grand.
Aunt Grainne, Uncle Bialas. The Ks.
Dana will be safe. She lives in the Witch Market.
What about Blathnat?
Please don't be near. Please don't have come.
Not tonight.
Not tonight.

Cleophas closes his eyes tightly. Inhales deeply. His terror is dropping his olfactory guards; the smells are getting to him. He can't lose his head now. The Xs will just find him when they leave.

He relaxes his eyelids. Breathes again. Exhales slowly. Clears his head.

His heart still booms.

He says a prayer, two prayers, three. His family must be safe. His friends must be safe. They must not be dead.

He needs to get into the Witch Market.

The south door is closest. But is it closed? How long has the extermination been going on? He doesn't own a watch.

He estimates he left the Cassiopeia at six fifteen. It must be at least six forty-five now. Maybe even later.

He steals a quick glance around the corner of the bakery.

The Xs are still moving about, but there are more of them now. As if they're coming back. Done.

They must be wrapping up the extermination.

They will be coming towards him soon.

He can't let them see him. But the south door must be closed. It might be open. But he can't take the chance if it's not. There are no chances here. One slight mistake and he will be dead before he hits the ground.

There are a few other ways into the Witch Market beside the doors. He doesn't know them all, but there's one that might work. One family, the Arandas, have a chute hidden in their tent that drops into the Witch Market.

Frantically, Cleophas wracks his brain. He has never used the Arandas' chute, never even seen it, but he knows their tent. It's not far from his own. It's big, and has a purple tarp on one side. A twisted metal pole sticks out from the roof.

The purple tarp and the pole. That's what he'll look for.

Cleophas takes another quick glance of the site. The Xs are starting to depart.

He'll have to leave the hoverbike behind. Maybe he'll be able to come back for it in a week or two. No one will be able to leave the Witch Market for a while.

He keeps the helmet on though. It will be his only piece of protection if an X sees him, but if it saves his life, so be it.

There is a small café up the road from the bakery Cleophas hides behind now. If he sprints, he can make it there in a few seconds, but he runs the risk of making noise. He creeps instead, taking quick, light steps until he ducks into the cover of the café. Cleophas darts to a large hole in the wall where a window once was and scans the space again, looking for the next available shelter.

He's trapped.

All the way from the café to the overpass there is nothing but roads and guardrails.

Nothing.

Empty space.

Cleophas's heart almost stops.

Save me.

The Xs are getting nearer. Their pods must not be far.

For a moment Cleophas wonders where the Xs landed them. He didn't see any on his way here.

Then he immediately drops to the tiled floor of the café, withdrawing into his cave of a coat. Frozen. He's never been so petrified.

Through a tall, thin crack at his eye level, Cleophas watches.

A figure stumbles from the buildings near him, oblivious to the Xs. As it walks further into the light, across the roads, Cleophas can see that it's a child. A little boy, about six or seven. He must have run into the crumbling streets when the Xs showed up.

Funny. They must not have been coming from this direction.

The boy moves across the roads, and Cleophas can see that the Xs have noticed.

This is what terrifies him.

The Xs do not move for a moment. Then one begins a steady approach. The others turn to leave. Now that they are clear of the overpass, they head up, away from the streets where Cleophas is hiding, to another part of old Boston.

Cleophas takes no notice.

His eyes are pinned to the little boy, who is calling for his mother.

His mother must be dead.

No parent would flee to the Witch Market without their child.

The lone X walks up to the boy, until they are within a few yards of each other. The boy has started to cry. He just stands there. Hopeless.

The X doesn't do anything. It just stands there too, in the dreaded yellow jumpsuit.

The child has noticed that he isn't dead yet. His crying softens, as he tries to work out what the X means to do.

The Boxians are not bad people. Foolish sometimes, but not bad.
Does that mean the Xs are not bad people?

Cleophas realizes he has been holding his breath. The child starts not to look so hopeless. Then the X speaks.

"What's your favorite color?"
And the bullet spits out of the boy's neck.

Cleophas closes his eyes. Tears squeeze from his eyes and he trembles inside that ridiculous coat, shivering, almost forgetting to breathe and swallow.

What's your favorite color?

It's a joke among the Xs, a death sentence for the Snitches. The Xs believe the Snitches are so animalistic that they have no souls. From souls comes creativity, of which color is a representative. If a Snitch can blurt out a color quickly enough, then they must possess a soul, and therefore should be spared, as they are obviously not a pest. Supposedly, years ago, a Snitch really could escape death in such a way, but that has long since become folly. The phrase carries no more meaning now than a death warrant and is used most commonly before the execution of children. Even if a color can escape a Snitch's lips in time, the X will already have pressed the orange button on the underside of their weapon, and the bullet will be on its chaotic trail of destruction through the victim's body.

Does that mean the Xs are not bad people?

Cleophas feels sick.

FOUR

An hour goes by before Cleophas finally uncurls from within his coat. Somewhere up above the sun has risen, giving what warmth and light it can force through the smog to BostonMaxia. Nothing escapes down here but the normal scraps of artificial light from Lower City, causing the transparent alumina supports to glow faintly as usual.

The tears that slid from Cleophas's eyes earlier have long since dried. The right side of his helmet, the one pressed against the floor of the café, is not even sticky.

The tiniest bit of salt twinges in Cleophas's nostrils, and he comes back around, breaking the black cocoon of his coat and exiting the café.

Cleophas was not watching when the X burned the boy's body. Now he steps over the ashes, fine and black.

What happens to the soul when the body dies?

The question makes him think of Blathnat.

He no longer fears for her death. Something tells him that

she has not been killed tonight.

The ashes do not smell like anything, which makes him sad.

In the ruin about and beyond the overpass, the scentless ash is everywhere. Some is scattered and stepped on, while some remains in the spots where the bodies fell. Tents and huts are broken and flattened, materials strewn across the site. Footprints are numerous, stamped over each other. Here and there are possessions: a mug, a couple of scans, a large polished stone.

Cleophas reaches Quillan's tent first. The Oddanies' tent is ripped and lopsided, one half drooping on the ground. Beneath the fallen tarps are two piles of ash. One is smaller than the other.

Cleophas kneels beside the two memorials. His eyes are wet and wide with shock. He knows the small pile belongs to one of the Ks, his darling cousins. The larger one could be his aunt, his uncle, or Quillan.

The footprints leaving directly from the tent are large. The Snitch that is now a pile of ash didn't make it. Aunt Grainne has small feet.

The Xs killed Quillan's mother. They killed one of the Ks.

A couple of tears skate down Cleophas's face.

In the mess of the tent he finds two water bottles and a pen. He empties what remains inside the bottles and fills them with the ashes. The pen he knows. He gave it to Quillan a few years ago for his birthday. He found it in Upper City. It's slim, but the emerald barrel is thick enough to grip comfortably, and it can write on anything. Cleophas writes a G on one bottle, a K on the other, and stows them both in his coat.

Beneath Quillan's cot is a small plastic box. In it are his most prized possessions. The pen is usually inside when Quillan doesn't have it with him, but Cleophas found it on the other side of the tent. Perhaps Uncle Bialas was using it last night and forgot to return it.

The box is not heavy, so Cleophas decides to take it with him. He probably would have lugged the thing to the Witch Market even if it weighed eighty pounds. He also picks up a link bracelet from the spot where he found the pen. It probably belonged to Aunt Grainne, but he can give it to one of the girls, whichever one he isn't carrying about inside his coat.

It takes next to no time to reach the Ektos' tent, and when he does Cleophas almost dies. Blood is spattered all over the tarps, and the tent is completely flat on the ground. Cleophas remembers seeing some bloodshed on the Oddanies' tent, but that is no amount compared to this. Despite the massive quantity of blood, there is only one pile of ash, lying just before the tent.

When Cleophas sees it, he falls to his knees, rips off the helmet and cries.

For some intuitive reason, he knows it's his mum.

Grainne's sister.

Brigitte.

Mum.

Mum.

Anguish melts over Cleophas, melts over him like mercury and lead and acid. Grief eats him up, pokes his hurts, gives him bruises. He feels tiny. He hunches over Quillan's box, the bottles bumping against his legs, blond hair pressed into the black ashes. He cries and chokes when he tries to inhale, until he rolls over, choking, swallowing strained, tight breaths, his eyes watering from tears and the fight for air.

Eventually he quiets. He's no longer convulsing for oxygen, but his face and neck are still wet with tears, his bandaged fingers shaking. The surrounding smells flood him, and this time he doesn't reapply his olfactory walls. In a few moments, the scents have overtaken his senses. Cleophas has surrendered to oblivion.

In the unconsciousness brought on by olfactory overload,

Cleophas does not dream; he relives.

*   *   *

The two of them lie beside each other on the roof of the bank. Down beneath the city the roof is cold, but they've been here many times. The bank rooftop is a favorite haunt. Jutting up out of the cracked sidewalk beside it is a transparent alumina abutment that spans the width of the road and scrapes against the side of the bank. It glows, mostly a light, colorless glow, but tinged faintly blue at the corners.

In the dimness, Cleophas speaks.

"Blathnat?"

"Mm?"

He likes saying her name. How the "th" letters vanish and continue the soft ah *sound. Blahnat, her name sounds like. He likes that.*

"What happens to the soul when the body dies?"

There's a silence, but nothing uncomfortable. Cleophas is in no hurry. Blathnat is thinking. The transparent alumina glows.

"I don't know," she says, "but, think this: Souls are good things."

Cleophas nods. They agreed on that during one of their previous conversations. Blathnat continues:

"It seems right that good things should always be good. They should always have good outcomes. The body gets beat up and dies eventually, and the soul's a bit hurt by that emotionally, more or

41

less so pertaining to the circumstances, but in the end, when the body's gone, the soul should be free. Free to always have good things."

"So goodness forever?"

"Yeah. In a way."

"Won't the soul get lonely? I mean, its home's gone. It's destroyed."

"Maybe it does get lonely. But just for a little bit. I think all the other free souls come and cheer it up."

"I like that."

"Me too."

They both ponder the matter for a while as the alumina glows. Cleophas thinks he hears it humming sometimes, but the sound disappears when he concentrates upon it, and he surmises that he probably just imagines the hum.

"I think they remember," he says.

"Remember the life in the body?"

"Yeah. Yeah, I think they do. Every bit. Even the bad stuff, the things that hurt."

"Maybe they can't forget."

"I don't think it would be good if they did. Because if they could forget, then they might choose just to remember the good things, and then it wouldn't matter if you're a soul with a body or without one. Bad things shape us just as much as good ones."

"They make us who we are."

"Exactly."

Bad things. There are so many bad things, Cleophas thinks. Especially in a Snitch's life. But there are also a lot of good things. Good times. Like now.

"Blathnat?"

"Mm?"

"Do you think souls cry?"

She takes a moment before answering.

"Yes, Cleophas. I think souls cry a lot."

He is quiet, calmly accepting the statement as fact. They both lay there, on the rooftop, still and unmoving, except for the soft swell and fall of their breasts. Blathnat's right hand finds Cleophas's left, and she grasps it gently, giving it a squeeze, which he returns. They hold hands in the dark, staring up at the roof of the cathedral that is old Boston. Beside the bank, the transparent alumina hums.

*　　*　　*

Cleophas regains consciousness. While he sets up his olfactory walls, there is one thought on his mind.

Souls cry a lot.

Oh, Mum.

His mother's soul is with Aunt Grainne's soul, and with one of the little girls; Klaudia or Kassia. He still does not know which is alive and which is in the bottle.

The souls are making each other feel better. His mum, his

aunt, his cousin. Cleophas doesn't like the thought of any one of them being lonely. It is better that they are together, to cheer each other up and give love and goodness.

There will be nothing but goodness now, Mum.

The lack of more ashes implies that Cleophas's father, Cleon, as well as his grandmother and great uncle have made it to the Witch Market. But Cleophas suspects that the blood is his father's and the question arises of if he is even alive. Cleophas skirts that thought. His father could be either dead or alive, judging by the amount of blood he's lost. There is no reason to dwell on the negative when there is no conclusive proof. He worries for his grandmother Lucinda and his great uncle, though. They are tough and weathered, but old. He hopes they have made it through.

Brigitte, Cleon, Gamma and Grand Nicodemus were the only ones home when the extermination began. His older sister, Helminette, had been in the Witch Market with her new husband, Redman.

Cleophas wonders if she knows their mother is dead.

He fills a screw top container with the ashes and stows it securely within his coat. He's glad he has the coat. He hugs it to himself for a moment, the ashes of three of his family held in its pockets, then goes about uncovering the wreckage of the tent.

Cleophas keeps most of his possessions on his person at all times, with the only exception being his other clothes, of which there are not many. He takes only extra underwear and socks for himself and devotes the remaining room in his coat to the property of his different family members. Helminette moved most of her belongings to her new home in the Witch Market, and Gamma and Grand keep many of their things in the Ektoses' house there as well, so the majority of the objects Cleophas takes belong to his parents.

Squashed into the ground is Brigitte's sewing kit. He takes that, as well as a small pouch containing a tiny mirror and a necklace of colored glass beads. Her wedding band disintegrated when she was burned. Like Cleophas, Brigitte kept many of her belongings attached to her. The wedding band is not the only thing Cleophas wishes he could have saved.

When he is done scouring the blood-stained remnants of his home, Cleophas has added the following to the growing inventory of his coat: A handwritten copy of John Keats' poem, *Bright Star*; an embroidered napkin, some golden ribbon, a scant handful of pens, a long knife with a battered sheath, a pouch of almond shavings, some drawings, half a loaf of bread, a bundle of incense sticks, a lighter; two glow-sticks, a small frying pan; five stackable cups, a hammer, and an old wooden beaver totem.

Cleophas puts the helmet back on his head. There is little use in wearing it now, but he can't leave it behind and there is nowhere else to put it. He checks over his coat, making sure everything is secured, steadily becoming accustomed to its new weight, then picks up Quillan's box and sets off towards the Arandas' tent.

It's a relief when he spies the purple tarp. He was worried it would have been unrecognizable and he wouldn't have been able to get into the Witch Market at all, but a small fire is burning nearby, and the tarp is well in the light.

The Arandas' tent is a large one, but it is almost untouched. The only spot disturbed is the entrance which is ripped as though people tried to force themselves inside. Cleophas goes in and immediately sees where the chute is. In one corner of the tent, the ground around a plastic mat is churned up with countless messy footprints. Cleophas lifts the mat to reveal the top of a metal chute. Sliding back the top, he sees the chute is round and about one yard in diameter. He'll fit easily.

First Cleophas presses Quillan's box against his chest and zips up his coat. Slowly, he puts his legs in the chute, then eases himself down until he is holding himself up by his fingers. There is a hooked rod on the bottom of the cover, and with one hand gripping a peg in the side of the chute, Cleophas slides the metal top shut. It closes with a click and

Cleophas is instantly submerged into absolute blackness. He tucks his coat close, folds his left arm around the box against his chest and takes a deep breath. Then he lets go of the peg and the drop down the chute begins.

It's not a long trip. The chute quickly changes from vertical drop to various different angles, and Cleophas just puts his head back and closes his eyes as he whooshes towards the Witch Market. In little more than a few minutes, the chute levels and comes to an end, and Cleophas shoots out onto hard-packed ground. The breath goes out of him with a little *uff* and he lies there for a few moments before unzipping Quillan's box from his coat. A few pats of the coat inform him that all its contents are in order. Then Cleophas gets to his feet and walks into the Witch Market.

FIVE

It is quiet in the Witch Market. All noise is low and indistinguishable, weaving a mat of fidgety activity. Cleophas treads steadily through the crooked streets, passing the dwellings of the secret community. There are houses down here in the Witch Market, not scrappy tents and huts like those that once stood about the overpass. They're small and shabbily put together, made of plastic and metal and cloth, but they're houses all the same. The narrow streets, thrown across the Witch Market like tracings of multiple doilies, are draped with strings of lights and beads and flags. Lines of paper lanterns crisscross overhead; spheres of green, ruby, purple, brown, and burnt umber. Totems and banners hang about doorways, sporadically bound with the odd string of dried plants or roots. Natural materials are difficult to come by nowadays, and the Snitches resort to stealing. The Witch Market's hothouse is one of its most prized elements.

The smells attach to Cleophas like moths to a lantern, following him. Incense and spices waft through the air, dominated by cinnamon, pepper, patchouli and licorice anise; the scents of cloves, frankincense and nutmeg are harder to discern. From the decrepit-looking houses are the smells of wax and paper, cracked leather, cotton and dust. Cleophas's nose detects the crumbs of old food, of honey and wine and dried tea, sugar, cooked meat, smoke and water. Sweat, salt and blood, as well as a stirring combination of age and youth are found in clouds around the Snitches; those that Cleophas sees about, and those that go unseen. Acrid metal, grit, coal, gas and dirt clog the air.

The smells are like tattoos, marking homes and places and people. Cleophas is used to the scents; he's grown up with them. All the individual stinks and aromas of multiple civilizations and cultures congregate to form one grouped smell: the bizarre, comforting scent of the Witch Market.

The Ektos house is roundish, made mostly from scrap metal. It is tucked in the hump of a crooked street, like a large copper teakettle, beaten and forgotten in the back of a cabinet. A trail of smoke coils out of a pipe on the roof. Light flickers through tiny cracks in the walls. Cleophas takes his helmet off and knocks briefly on the door before letting himself in. There is a great flurry of movement; shadows are thrown around the room and faces are a haze. Cleophas is snatched up in the arms of an elderly woman. His Gamma, Lucinda, holds him tightly to her rail of a body; Cleophas can feel her shaking as he buries his face in her shoulder. She smells of terror and relief at the same time, of age and sadness and experience.

The room, though the largest in the house, is still a small one, and it seems tiny now, stuffed with the people of Cleophas's life. Grand Nicodemus, his great uncle, sits in a chair beside the gas-powered stove, the light etching dark lines into his worn, wrinkled face. On the other side of the stove, in the shadows, is Cleophas's Aunt Karin; Brigitte and Grainne's sister. In her dim position, her features are unreadable.

Lucinda releases Cleophas from her hold and he sees the other occupants clearly. Uncle Bialas is sitting at the table like a statue; Kassia, his surviving daughter is curled up in his lap, and with a heavy heart Cleophas finally knows which of his cousins is in a plastic bottle in his coat.

Quillan's Aunt Yeva sits beside Bialas. At the other end of the table are Dana's brother and uncle, Fontaine and Darcy. Her parents, Dante and Alverdine, are standing behind them along the wall.

"Where are they?" Cleophas asks. "Quillan and Dana?"

"At our home," says Dante, his arm around Alverdine's waist. "Recuperating."

"What about my father?"

"He's here," says Lucinda. "He's resting. He got shot."

Cleophas nods numbly. He picks up Quillan's box and sets it down on the table. To make up for the lack of words in his mouth, he sits and starts pulling objects from his coat. The bottles and the screw-top container sit in a wretched row before he pushes Aunt Grainne's and Klaudia's ashes towards Bialas, placing the bracelet beside them for Kassia. When Bialas does not make any motion or expression, Kassia grabs them, holding the bottles close in her skinny arms. She looks at her father with scared concern, until Yeva gets to her feet. She's a large woman, solidly built with a stalwart and bolstering demeanor, and it is with care that she puts a hand on her brother's shoulder.

"Come on," she says, "you're staying with me today."

When Bialas does not stir, her gentle touch becomes a grip.

"Bialas. Get up."

The edge of urgency in her voice coaxes him to his feet. Kassia is the only person he seems to be aware of; he carries her like a child younger than her years, her limbs wrapped around him like a monkey's. A bandage is bound around Bialas' left calf. It is already blooming with red roses, but Bialas seems oblivious to any pain. As Yeva reaches for Quillan's box, Cleophas puts a hand on it.

"I'll get it to him," he says, and there is a pleading undertone in his voice that Yeva recognizes.

"Thank you," she says, saying more in two words than

she would have in twenty, before following Bialas out of the door.

"How is my father?" Cleophas asks the quiet room, continuing to empty his coat onto the table.

"He's badly injured," Nicodemus says. "The Xs shot him after they killed your mother. The only reason he's alive is because the ones shooting him weren't using button guns. Some different weapon with cruder bullets."

"Is he going to be all right?"

"He'll live, but he won't be moving extensively any time soon."

"Can I go see him?"

"Best leave him be right now, love," Lucinda tells him gently. "Later, perhaps this evening."

"I want to let him know I'm here—"

"But you weren't."

Cleophas's gaze snaps to his Aunt Karin's. Her eyes flash like a knife turned over and her voice has a bite.

"You weren't there when it happened and you're lucky to be here now. Your parents were worried sick. Brigitte was going ballistic because no one knew where you were. They thought you were dead, or already fried to steaming ashes—"

"Karin—" Dana's father interrupts.

"This isn't your family, Dante, don't pretend you have some pass into this conversation," Aunt Karin snaps, not tearing her gaze from Cleophas, the venom in her voice broiling. "You'd gone Up again, hadn't you? No matter how many times you're told not to, you still go Up. Spying on the ridiculous, hoity-toity people above, watching their habits and smelling them like a doped bloodhound, it's no wonder they hate us —"

"Karin," Dante says sharply. "It is not Cleophas's fault that Brigitte died."

Karin looks at Dante in shock, words knotting in her mouth. When it becomes apparent that the topic is closed for discussion, her jaw sets in a pained scowl and she strides out of the house, her dark blonde hair flowing around her face.

"Does Helminette know?" Cleophas asks. His voice is very small.

"Yes," Lucinda says.

"Did she ever come by, to see Dad?"

"She stayed with Redman. She'll come by later, when the shock has worn off some."

Cleophas feels the room unfold as his Gamma finds new homes for the items he salvaged. Helminette has not been round. She's been growing further and further apart from the family ever since her marriage and Cleophas misses her company dreadfully. He wants her now, just for her to *be* here, to give him something to feel more secure about.

"I'm off," Darcy interjects into the silence, getting up from the table.

"We should head out too," says Dante, looking at Fontaine, who relinquishes his chair.

Cleophas is glad the Creares and the Oddanies have come. The three families are so close-knit they might as well be one. Fontaine is like an older brother to Cleophas; he even has some degree of love for Darcy and Aunt Karin, despite their abrasive personalities. Aunt Karin in particular is rough around the edges. She has always been the toughest of her sisters; Cleophas has never seen her display the same level of kindness as Brigitte or Grainne. Their deaths have only hardened her further.

"Can I come with you?" Cleophas asks, slipping his arm around Quillan's box.

Dante nods an affirmative and Cleophas kisses Lucinda on the cheek.

"I'll be back later," he tells her.

Darcy departs before they reach the Creares' house, disappearing down another street to his own home. Of their families, Darcy is one of the people Cleophas knows the least. He has always been a reclusive, shadowy figure.

The Creare house is one of the larger houses in the Witch Market and it has a more put-together look, constructed of bent sheets of metal and steel beams. The house even has a second floor. This place is familiar to Cleophas. The house is dominated by the scent of books and thick paper and old ink, tinged with the rank odor of chemicals, spicy liquids, and powder that permeates from Dana's room. All of this mingles with the dusty, white-wine tinged scent of Dante, and the flowery, honeyed smell Cleophas associates with Alverdine. She's a tall woman, slender and attractive, with long dark hair brushed back from her face and sparkling green eyes beneath trim brows. Cleophas used to have a crush on her when he was much younger; a shy, childish admiration he has long since outgrown.

The main room is large and angular; the walls are lined with shelves of books and ledgers. Maps and other various texts are pinned up in layered patches, like swathes of papery dragon scales. Dante sinks into a chair, rifling through an open file as Alverdine disappears into the kitchen, beckoning to Fontaine to come help her.

"They're in Dana's room," Dante says.

Cleophas nods. He shouldn't be long.

As Cleophas enters Dana's bedroom, the dingy chemical smell increases, interspersed with the scents of vinegar and wine. Unlike her father, Dana prefers red. She drinks occasionally when she's working.

Dana's companion animal, an eastern screech owl named

Hewett, roosts on a shabby leather perch across from the door. The bird's eyes blink open, large and round. Musty bird-scent surrounds him.

Hewett was discovered by Dante several years ago, flapping throughout old Boston. No one knows how the owl got down there, or what it was doing, but it took a shine to Dante and followed him back to the Witch Market, despite Dante's many attempts to get the bird to leave. He ended up presenting Hewett to Dana as a sort of birthday present, but Hewett has become more of a friend than a pet. Dana likes his presence.

Dana and Quillan are lying on Dana's bed, fully clothed and sound asleep. Dana is laying on her left, keeping the pressure off her injured leg, and her back is to the wall, one arm slung protectively over Quillan's waist. In sleep, her face loses the fierceness she usually wears and her expression is gentle and young. Quillan is curled up against her, his back to her stomach, chocolaty-auburn curls brushing Dana's cheek in swirls. His left hand is heavily bandaged.

Cleophas watches them quietly, unmoving. Their breathing is synchronized, their lips parted slightly. Cleophas sets Quillan's box down on Dana's work table, amongst her test tubes and papers and mortars and the electric stick she is building. His eyes water as he wipes away a spot of mustard seed and he chokes and sneezes sharply. His attention darts to his friends on the bed, but they are still and undisturbed. Hewett blinks at him, shuffling his clawed feet on his perch. Cleophas hesitates a moment, then leaves. He thought he'd feel close and comfortable in the company of his friends, but instead he feels strangely lonely.

In the main room, Dante is reading a battered copy of *War and Peace*. Cleophas can smell cooked grease and fat wafting out from the kitchen; Fontaine is frying sausages and bread. Alverdine appears in the doorway, a mug nestled between her palms.

"Are you staying for breakfast, Cleophas?"

Dante looks up from his book.

"No, thank you, I should go home," Cleophas says.

"Do you want a cup of tea before you leave?"

"I'm fine, really, thank you," he says, excusing himself.

Walking back to his house, he wishes that Blathnat would appear at a random corner. The feeling of loneliness is encasing him, weighing on his shoulders, sinking into the folds of his coat. Quillan and Dana are as close as family to him; closer, in certain respects. They understand him differently. Despite this, as much as he loves them, the sight of the two of them together, so utterly contingent to each other, leaves him feeling isolated.

How he wishes to catch sight of Blathnat beneath one of

the colored lanterns; her skin painted green or violet or red. He wants her scent to fill his nostrils; she always smells faintly of smoke, but stronger of daffodils, due to a perfume she wears. When her fingers smell of fish scales, he knows she's been in the Asian market in Lower Boston, where every breath of air is loaded with grease and the stench of fish guts. Her feet smell like carrots. He's never been able to figure that out. He can tell what food she's last eaten by smelling it on her lips; sometimes its watercress, sometimes its pumpkin, sometimes its rice or mint or spicy black bread. Her hair smells like the blue chemical dye she puts in it. It's always loose around her face, except for the one braid strung with wooden beads painted green and yellow.

She's beautiful. Such a beautiful, liberated soul. Her body is terpsichorean and lissome; Cleophas loves the way she moves. She walks lightly, her footsteps like petals of smoke curling up from the earth. Her hair fans out behind her in a blue sheet when she runs, swelling around her face in a cloud when she swivels her long neck to look back for him. Her eyes are golden, soft and bright, like antiquated coins that have changed hands many times over. They wink at him, laughing and smiling.

SIX

Lucinda and Nicodemus are sitting at the table drinking tea when Cleophas walks in. He notices the container filled with his mother's ashes has been untouched, while everything else he brought back has been put away, placed on shelves or inside boxes and cabinets.

The two elderly people are quiet and Cleophas does not speak as he sits down with them. Lucinda puts a mug before him and he accepts it, wrapping his bandaged fingers around its belly, ignorant of the scalding heat. He takes a drink, gulping down the liquid and burning his mouth. The bitter, lemony flavor splits open on his tongue. He presses his forehead against the tabletop, nostrils flaring as he ingests the thin, plastic smell. His eyes shut, he feels Nicodemus grasp his hand firmly.

"You shouldn't have gone Up, Son."

Grand squeezes his hand, and despite the reprimand, Cleophas knows he is forgiven.

The Ektoses' house belongs to Gamma Lucy and Grand

more than anyone else in the family. Cleophas and his sister Helminette grew up among the tents outside the Witch Market on their mother's insistence. Brigitte had always found the Witch Market too claustrophobic, and it was she who used to walk with Cleophas through the ruins of old Boston, speaking animatedly of cathedrals and architecture and the velvetiness of the dark while he held her hand in awe.

But the tent is gone now, and the Ektoses' house is a bit of home. The inside looks like the interior of a brass pepper pot; cozy, round and warm, like a belly filled with tea and jam. It is smaller than Dana's house, with less clutter. The kitchen is combined with the fore room to create a large, singular living space. Every object is tucked neatly in its place. The cupboards and shelves lining the walls are straight and orderly. The gas-powered stove is small and looks misfit, but is kept clean and tidy. Candles are stuck to most surfaces, their plastic throats singed black at the top where they have melted from their own heat. A framed, brightly colored map of Greece and the Mediterranean Sea hangs beside the spice cabinet, while intricate watercolors of Notre Dame and the Basilica of Sacré Cœur overlook the water basin and tub that serve as a sink. Three crocheted quilts adorn the walls, the products of Lucinda's busy hands. An indigo quilt hangs near the door. The largest one is a faded green color, encompassing the tiny kitchen. The smallest quilt is hung on the wall behind the stove, like a cherry-red spider's web.

Beyond, in one of the bedrooms, is Cleophas's father. Cleophas takes another gulp of tea.

"Can I see him now?"

Cleon Ektos lays outstretched in bed, his abdomen heavily bandaged beneath a clean shirt. Whatever bleeding there was has stopped enough so that the bandages are stained pink, rather than red. He looks older than his forty-seven years, with bags under his eyes and hollow cheeks. There is more salt in his brown hair than there was yesterday, Cleophas notices. His father's eyes latch onto his with unexpected vigor. Cleon has gray eyes like his son, one of the only common features between them, but while Cleophas's eyes are like pale gray pearls, Cleon's are stormy.

"I thought they killed me for a moment," Cleon says, as Cleophas sits down on a stool at the bedside.

"Does it hurt?"

Of course it hurts.

"I'm on morphine. Leon patched me up."

"When did they get Mum?"

"Not long after we caught sight of them. She wanted to go looking for you."

Cleon eyes his son from behind a mask, half scowling, half apathetic.

"She didn't think they'd got you, you know. She kept going on about how you'd keep away from it all. But she was worried. She wanted to get you before they did, in case you finally drew the short straw.

"You went Up."

Penitence is fashioning a black necklace around Cleophas's throat. He nods.

"Dammit, Cleo!" his father says abruptly, thumping his fist on the mattress. His face is twisted up in a strange mixture of pain, anger, and unreleased grief. Cleophas can see it hanging off his neck like an albatross, and he feels a very internal ache starting to bubble up in his stomach, bending a budding head like a blossom that cannot quite force itself upright. Cleon has never called him Cleo before. That was Brigitte's name for him.

For a while, neither of them speaks. Nor do they look at each other. Cleophas studies the scrappy bandages on his hands. He should change them; they're dirty and are starting to smell stale. He's never careful enough around the steam from the ventilation grates; it's likely he'll burn his hands again soon.

Cleophas has never felt as close to his father as he was to Brigitte. Cleon has always been harder; he's a physical being. He intimidates Cleophas, with his strong, extroverted nature and volatile temper. He is not a mean man, Cleophas knows this, but he is unpredictable and grounded, like a dormant volcano. Dana has always gotten on well with him; they share a vision of a changing future and appreciate practical actions. Cleophas has always been more thoughtful and distant, ever the observer, and Cleon cannot grasp that. He worries over his boy, for he doesn't know how to keep tabs on him.

Cleophas fiddles with his pockets and his fingers stumble over the beaver totem he retrieved from the tent. He pulls it out, grimy fingertips brushing over the wood polished smooth by age and handling. It belongs to his father, and he holds it out to him in his palm.

"Keep it, Cleophas. You might as well have something of mine."

The words sting unexpectedly.

"Go on out, Cleophas. Go do something."

Cleophas is almost out of the room when his father says, "I shouldn't have to remind you, but the doors are closed. We're going to be shut in for a while, so don't even think of finding a way out. This isn't a time to be going Up."

*   *   *

The front door, the south door, is shut.

It's a massive construction, the south door; fourteen inches of solid steel, twenty-five feet wide and sixteen feet high. A row of spikes protrude from the bottom, sinking into the locking mechanisms beneath the metal plating that covers the ground. This is the main entrance to the Witch Market. There are is one smaller door, the north door, but this is the one most often used.

Cleophas is already feeling contained, pacing in slow steps in front of the door. While he doesn't mind being in the Witch Market, he likes having the freedom to come and go as he chooses, and having that taken from him makes him tense. He knows other ways in and out of the Witch Market, small, secret ways, but he shouldn't use them. Not now, under these circumstances. He feels like a butterfly caught in a glass jar. He can see the holes in the top where he could escape, but he can't use them. The sense of protection he normally feels at the south door is not present; there's oppressiveness instead.

How he wants to see Blathnat, he thinks, trailing his fingers delicately along the door. How he wants to smell her skin again. All he can smell here beside the door are the echoes of fear and old blood. He can smell the speed that the Snitches rushed with like shadows. They are bitter smells, unfriendly, unfeeling.

The last time he saw Blathnat, their encounter was fleeting. She was rushing through a heavily scented street of the Witch Market, her pockets bulging with globs of spices and oils. Her blue hair was pulled back under a hood, strands of it seeping free to dangle around her long, beautiful face.

"Blathnat!"

She turns, swiveling like a dancer, and yet still reminding him of the clips of gazelles he has seen on tablets, head high and alert.

"Where are you going?" Cleophas asks, once he reaches her.

"I have to go out." She's agitated. He can smell it on her, under the spices in her pockets. It's a sharp smell on Blathnat. Cleophas's eyes crinkle, trying to deduce her frame of mind. "Cleophas, I can't stay. I have to go."

He takes her hand and she returns, drawing close to him. He has to look up to meet her eyes. Golden, and he sees the familiar softness there. She kisses him, capturing his mouth with her tender lips. Cleophas is overcome with the scent of her. The musty touch of the hood on his face; the smoke in her hair; the freshness of daffodils on her skin, beneath all other scents. The daffodil perfume is embedded in her; Blathnat is always in the springtime of her life. He can taste pumpkin and wheat in her mouth, sugar on her tongue and teeth. All over is the earthy aroma that can only be called Blathnat smell.

Her lips move slowly against his, like crocus petals opening in winter light. Something young, something old, something new, something deep. I love you, *the kiss says.* I care about you.

Words pass between them, communicated through the alignment of their lips. There is always time for you. You are not forgotten.

They have always understood each other, always had an

intuitive, unspoken connection. This contact, so old, so new, is an affirmation.

She left after the kiss, Cleophas's heart thudding as he watched her go. He was concerned, for her- agitation is unusual for her character- but the kiss had calmed him. He felt gratified, secure. Everything was in its place.

Cleophas relaxes thinking of the encounter. He sits down, leaning against the south door, hands clasped around his knees. Tilting his head up, he looks at the ceiling of the Witch Market; a great expanse of concrete infused with rivers of transparent alumina, like a ghostly spider web. The scattered light of the Witch Market quickly bleeds into darkness, soft and velvety like the roof of old Boston. Closing his eyes, Cleophas imagines that he is walking those forgotten streets with his mum again. Brigitte holds his hand in hers, warm and close, and together they stare up into the darkness.

SEVEN

Quillan wakes gradually, his eyes blinking slowly as though he has been sedated. His left hand is numb. He feels Dana pressed along his back, their bodies perfectly slotted together. Her right hand is draped over his ribcage, resting unclenched on his chest. He looks at her hand sleepily, tracing the paths and joints of her fingers. Her hand is so much softer in sleep. Not busy, not hard, not rough or stubborn or angry. It looks gentle, curled lax against his heart.

Gingerly, he twists around, taking care not to put any pressure on his left hand, until he is lying facing Dana. She's a little higher up on the bed, her head resting on the pillow. Her face is so calm and quiet. The edge so often present in her waking expression is nowhere to be found. Quillan warms as he looks at her. It's not often that he sees her so restful.

Her skin is browner than his, thanks to Dante. The warm Italian and Spanish tones harmonize with her curls, mussed and tangled. Her hair is flat where her head is pressed into the pillow, the low light making it appear several shades darker. Where the light of Dana's lamp touches her hair, it shines like molasses.

Her round face looks almost cherubic in sleep; her lips fuller, her nose sweeter and more upturned. A few little ringlets have escaped the ratty red bandana she uses to manage her curls, falling around her cheeks. Her lashes are thin and dark. There are freckles on her eyelids; flecks of cinnamon.

Quillan lays his right hand on her chest above her breasts, listening to her breathe as he watches the part in her mouth, listening to her sleep. It's magnetizing, and he feels hypnotized, following her slow inhales and exhales, moving in the wake of the undulations of her life. So soft. So soft.

There is a hitch in Dana's breath, and she opens her eyes. Her pupils are large in the brown shadows. He can hardly make out the blue of her eyes.

"Hello," he says.

Her right hand slowly curls against the back of his neck, thumb brushing the water-like swirls of hair that taper at his nape. Her left closes over the hand on her breasts, fingers sheathing it. Quillan palms his enveloped hand tenderly against her breasts and leans up to kiss her, his neck arcing back into her touch as she meets his mouth.

Quillan can never get tired of kissing Dana. The way their lips mold together, the warmth traveling between their bodies, the flush that appears in their skin. Her fingers press into the nape of his neck.

Hello.

The hand wrapped around his, the one pressing against her breasts, tightens, and Dana parts her lips against Quillan's ever so slightly.

"I want to be close to you," she says.

Quillan slowly runs his fingers over her shirt, pressing a gentle kiss to the side of her mouth. Keeping his bandaged hand close to his chest, he wraps his other arm around Dana's waist and slowly maneuvers them into a sitting position. Laying a kiss against her neck, Quillan pulls her shirt up over her stomach and breasts. Dana adds her hands, removing it entirely, and unhooks her bra, dropping it to the side. Quillan kisses his way down her neck and clavicle as Dana unties his shirt, working it off his shoulders and down his arms. Her hands align on either side of his neck as Quillan kisses her breasts, mouthing her skin with wet, velvet movements. He can hear Dana's heart, feel it through her skin, hear the music of her breathing above his head, the air that passes through her open mouth.

He lays his injured hand against her back as he bends, kissing the curve of her waist, his right hand sliding between her trousers to cup her hip. Dana moves her hands down his chest, her fingers trailing across the muscles beneath his skin.

She buries her face in his hair and he can feel her inhaling his scalp, absorbing the tracks of his brain. Quillan kisses her waist openly, hugging the curve with his lips. The two of them work together to maneuver her body so that Dana is lying on her back. Quillan bends over her from the side, juggling both their maladies as he kisses his way down her navel. Dana's hands frame his face, and he pulls up to look at her as she unbuttons her pants, lifting her hips to pull them down. Her eyes are dark and blue, so dark, her mouth parted like a rose, her breasts falling to the sides as she lies. Quillan moves up her body and meets her again, resting his weight on his elbows as he kisses her, lips spread like a book. Dana continues to administer to their remaining clothes, and soon Quillan is sitting back, working their pants and underwear off their ankles.

He presses gentle kisses to Dana's hip, crouched between her legs, her hands wrapped in his hair. He kisses his way softly up her stomach, taking his time as he bends his body and shifts into her. He clutches Dana as she inhales a cloud, his forehead pressed against her sternum. Her fingers massage the sides of his head, running through the curls above his ears, and she guides him up. Arms supporting each other, they twist to the side, lying on Quillan's right. His right leg intertwines with her left, and their hips lock together as they fall into their familiar position, the one that best accommodates Dana's mangled leg.

Quillan hooks his right arm beneath her, drawing Dana up higher. They meet at a comfortable angle, bodies aligned. Their foreheads touch for a moment before their lips brush lightly again, a prelude to longer, richer kisses. The rhythm between them is slow and weighted, ebbing and flowing the way the sea sucks on sand.

Their lungs are synchronized, bodies working together to achieve a comforting harmony. Dana breathes into the damp crook of Quillan's neck, her hands clutching his shoulder blades as he moves them back and forth, one hot instrument. Quillan's bandaged hand lies between Dana's breasts, his right hand cradling the back of her head. His fingers are laced among the mussed curls, lips soft against her ear.

When their movements have eased and Dana's fingernails have stopped pressing half-moons into Quillan's back, they lay still, breaths quiet. Quillan's eyes are shut, his face pressed into Dana's neck, lips parted. He can taste the sweat on her skin, feel the thrum of the heat between their thighs. Her heartbeat is softer now, recovering from its excited track, back to pushing blood through her body. So steady. So sure.

Dana's hands caress his back, one making its way up his head to stroke his hair. She moves her hand down to rest against his cheek. Her eyes are blue, blue like midnight, her cheeks rosy. She looks so soft.

I'll take care of you.

He isn't sure which of them says it, but that doesn't matter; they both mean it.

He holds his injured hand over her heart, closing his eyes, wrapped in her heat and listening to her breathe.

EIGHT

Quillan sits on her workbench wearing his pants, looking at her with his big light brown eyes. Dana can tell he's feeling slightly uncomfortable. The impact of the extermination is settling on him, sinking in like snow, but that's not all.

Dana represses a sigh. How has she ended up with him? How is it that she has this man wrapped around her finger? The way he looks at her; so much care, so much devotion. She twists her fingers around a bit of her hair, her arm brushing against her bare breast. The bedclothes are bunched on her lap. They fell asleep after having sex, and Dana woke first this time. It's still early, only around ten a.m. according to Dana's clock, but time feels irrelevant. There's tension spreading between the two of them, the familiar tension that always seems to be present when they're awake. The unity they share during sex doesn't carry over to their daytime relationship. Dana runs a hand through her messy hair. She's not looking at Quillan anymore, but she can feel his endearing, afterglow eyes. Dana knows Quillan finds her alluring and attractive.

He's always been sensual, and he loves intimacy. Dana enjoys it too, but she rarely lingers in the afterglow. Dana's brain is like a laboratory. When she's awake, she goes to work.

Dana's mentality is partly borne of the Witch Market. When one is a Snitch, one has to think practically to be successful and survive. Dana isn't one to linger on sentiment; she's too pragmatic. The open and flexible nature she has during sex rarely bleeds into the rest of her life.

"We should tell Iris about Tancred," Quillan says, breaking the ice. He's not looking directly at her anymore.

"She probably already knows," Dana replies.

"I still want to tell her. I want to talk with her, tell her how Tancred saved me."

"If you want."

"They were going to get married," Quillan says softly, studying his hands.

Dana starts getting dressed, looking around the bed for her underwear.

"When is this going to stop, Dana?"

For a moment, Dana almost freezes, thinking that he means them. Then she realizes what he's talking about.

"It can't just stop, Quillan. That's not how the world works." She's found her underwear. "The Xs will keep coming. We'll keep dying. But we live on. We survive." *Where's my bra?* "We develop. We grow. We keep finding new ways to protect ourselves."

"But we don't, Dana," Quillan says quietly. "We're too slow. The exterminations come out of nowhere; we never have a warning."

"That's exactly it, though. We have to make progress. That's what's at the core of this whole lifestyle. We have to make big changes, take chances to protect what's ours."

"Dana, you know I'm all for protection and conservation, but what more can we do?"

He's getting agitated.

"Continue with defenses, keep quiet, don't go Up, move everyone living on the outside into the Witch Market, but what else? What kind of risk are you talking about?"

"We should move the Witch Market," Dana says, snapping on her bra.

"And how do you propose we do that?" Quillan says, incredulous.

"We'd need people to look outside of Boston, for starters. There's no point in preparing if we have nowhere to go."

"You can't be serious."

Dana gives Quillan a long look.

"It's perfectly reasonable, Quillan."

"No, it's not! Move the Witch Market? Are you crazy? We can't just pick it up and drop it down somewhere else."

"Well, obviously, it's more complicated than that."

"I can't believe you're actually considering this."

Dana tugs her shirt over her head and levels with him.

"The Xs are getting closer. We all know that. Eventually, they'll decide to pursue us into the Witch Market. They will find a way in. We can build defenses and try to maintain them but not forever; we don't have the materials. Our weaponry is a scrap yard. Defense isn't the only thing we're short of. Our resources are dwindling. There's only so much we can scavenge from Lower City, and not many take the idiot's chance and go Up. We may be dying, but our population is increasing. How many babies were born last year? Sixteen? We're running out of oil, out of gas. Every bit of wood we have is practically gone. Our food is depleting again, and water can only be spread so thin. We'll kill ourselves eventually if we don't find an alternative.

"Moving the Witch Market is the most logical solution. It will be difficult, but it can be done. Once we find a location, we can leave in small groups, small enough to be undetected.

"We haven't acknowledged it, Quillan, but we're running out of time. This is what we've come to."

Quillan is silent for a while. Dana can't see his face; he's staring at the floor, bent over.

"This is our home."

Dana wants to shake him.

"But we can't stay here."

"We'll die if we leave. There's no way we can smuggle a thousand people out of the city."

"We'll die if we stay."

"You can't be certain of that!" Quillan is angry. It's a rare change from his gentle temperament.

"But it's true, Quillan!" Dana erupts. "You just don't want to believe it. You think everything will be fine as long as we stay down here, as long as we keep living like scum, never seeing proper sunlight, never breathing clean air, rationing out food because we can hardly grow anything edible at all. Despite the fact that there are people up there who don't think of us as human beings, despite the fact that there are people who come down out of nowhere to kill *children* — yes, it will all be fine. We'll be safe, safe in our own prison, until we're finally all killed or dead from starvation."

"What if you get pregnant?" Quillan says, getting to his feet.

"What?" She hasn't expected this angle.

"We just had unprotected sex, Dana. What if you get pregnant? What if you have a baby? Would that change your view on any of this?"

"We've had unprotected sex before."

"Yes, and we're lucky that you never conceived. But what if you do? What if this is the time? Would you still want to try to move out of the Witch Market? This place is the only bit of security we have."

"That's hypothetical," Dana snaps. "I don't know if I'm pregnant. We just had sex an hour or so ago, damn it."

"But what if you are?" Quillan kneels in front of her, pleading. He puts his hands in her lap, but she pushes them away. "What if it's now?"

What if it's now.

That's a hell of a lot of weight.

"Do you want to have a family?" Dana asks, point-blank.

"I love you," Quillan says, as if that answers everything.

"Do you want to have a family?" she repeats.

"Dana—"

"Give me something concrete, Quillan."

"I do. Eventually. At some point, yes."

"And do you want that some point to be now?"

"Hypothetically—"

"Hypothetically!" Dana says angrily, "You were the one who started spewing "what if"s. You say you want a family. Do you know how naïve you sound? Yes, you say, yes, I'd like a family. Eventually. At some point. Oh, Dana, are you pregnant? Hooray, wonderful, that's a nice surprise.

"So, *hypothetically*, what if I am pregnant? Are you suddenly all set to be a father, to devote your all? Do you know how much responsibility a baby is?"

Quillan's face has darkened.

"I do, actually. I had sisters, in case you've forgotten. Now I only have one. I helped raise them for nine years. I loved them with every ounce of my body. I still do. Don't ask me questions like that, Dana, because you have no clue what I've been through. I only have Kassia now, and I have to be her whole world, because one parent is dead and the other one is so disconnected from life that I have to take care of him, too. So don't ask me about responsibility and act like I'm a foreigner to it, because I have more than my fair share and I take care of all of it."

Dana recoils. It was insensitive of her to say that, but she's not in a state to adhere to Quillan's emotions. They're both angry, and Dana can't help but keep feeding the flame between them.

"How long have you wanted this?"

"How long have I wanted what?" Quillan exclaims, getting to his feet again. "A family? I don't know, Dana. I love you. I love you so much. I want to spend the rest of my life with you, I want to make things with you, I want to take care of you, I want to have kids with you and I want to have sex with you and kiss you and sleep next to you every night. I want us to stop pretending to be enemies all the time. I want us to be able to relax around each other when we're not having sex. I want to be able to call your family my family, which I practically already do. I want to be able to come over to your house not just to talk to Dante about literature and Spanish and Latin. I want to watch you work with your explosives and chemicals. I want to make you breakfast and lunch and dinner, I want to stay in bed with you all day, I want to read to you and talk to you in Spanish about our bad days and our good days and I want to wake up next to you every day for the rest of my life. It's a lot. There's a lot."

"We have sex, Quillan —"

"We have sex? Is that it?" Quillan yells, but he is cringing, his voice and face twisted in pain. Hewett squawks on his perch, shuffling his wings. "Don't try to hide how you feel from me, Dana, it doesn't work. I know you. You know me. You care about me as much as I care about you, but you do a damn good job of making me doubt that. I love you, Dana."

"I love you, too!" Dana screams at him, wishing more than ever that she could stand up without a support. "I fucking love you, are you happy? I do, I fucking do, but this is difficult, it's all difficult —"

"What?"

"THIS." Dana gestures, throwing her arms open wide, "All of this! You! Dealing with you and everything you wish and want. I don't know if I want a family, Quillan that's why I said we have sex because that's what we DO. I fucking love you, but I don't know if I can do that, everything you said about a family and how you took care of the Ks, I just can't do

82

that right now! Shut UP, *HEWETT!*"

The owl has been flapping around the room agitatedly, hooting. Dana lunges over to her door and pulls it open, falling to the floor as Hewett flies out. She falls on her bad leg and cries out in pain. Quillan instantly drops at her side, trying to help her, but she shoves him away.

"Go away, Quillan! Just — go away."

"Dana, please — I'm sorry, please —"

"GET OUT."

Dante is sitting in his armchair when Dana emerges from her room, crutch tucked into her armpit. She maneuvers the various crates and contorted furniture that clutter the main room, moving to sit down on a step ladder near one of the bookcases. Dante puts aside *War and Peace,* laying his arms loosely on the armrests. The house is quiet.

"Where's Hewett?"

"He went outside as soon as you let him out. Your mother left at the same time."

"And Fontaine?"

"He went out earlier. Seems he abides by the domestics' forecast more than the rest of us do."

They don't have to talk about it. Dante heard it all anyway, at least the shouting. He's accustomed to their antics. All the same, they've never had a fight like that before. Dana still feels cold and shielded. Her guards are thrown up on every side, and she feels like she's protecting some cringing creature inside her chest, defending it with anger and sharpness.

Dante's immune to her aggression. Somehow, it just brushes off of him, as insubstantial as air. Dana knows she's more like Dante than Alverdine. Her mother has English fae in her; she's a soft, earthy woman, fragile and gentle. Dana has fire and mettle and an ox-strong nerve. Dante is the reef that Dana's anger breaks on, keeping it at bay. He understands her.

"Do you think we're doing the right thing?"

"That's a very broad statement, coming from you," Dante replies.

"Staying here, in the Witch Market. Do you think it's wise?"

Dante muses for a moment then gets to his feet, collecting spare dishes from around the room and bringing them into the kitchen.

"We've only got white wine," he calls back to her. "Will that do?"

"It'll have to," she says.

Dante reenters with a little glass in each hand, leaning over a crate of yellowing papers to give one to Dana.

"Last of that bottle," he says, sitting back down. "Cheers."

"You shouldn't drink so much of it," Dana says

reproachfully, taking a gulp and scowling at the taste.

"Says you, who drinks a bottle of red a day," Dante retorts. "You drink more of it than anyone else down here. You do realize we'll run out of it sooner rather than later."

Dana shrugs, taking another sip of the dry white wine.

"We'll run out of everything eventually. But I'm sure you know that," Dante says pointedly.

They've come back to her question. Dana loves it when he does this. All of their conversations are the same; there is a precise order to them, and each movement is perfectly executed.

"The question is, what do we do about it?" Dante says, tapping his fingers on the armrest. "We are increasing, albeit slowly, and our resources are steadily trickling away."

"So why are we still here?" Dana asks lowly.

"Because this is what we have," Dante replies, his voice calm. "This is what we know. This," he gestures airily around them, "is all we have. We stay because we must."

"Or so we believe," Dana interjects.

"Or so we believe." Dante agrees. "Now, is it wise? That's an interesting question. It's understandable, certainly. Look around; we're all terrified. We want security, and we'll cling to whatever security the Witch Market can provide us. But is that a wise decision? That question leads us in other directions; we begin to look at our options. So what do we have?"

"We leave," Dana says simply.

"We leave the Witch Market."

"Yes. We scout, we find a new location, we uproot, and little by little, we leave."

"No more Xs."

"Exactly. No more Xs, no more limitations, no more starving, no more unnecessary deaths. Freedom."

That's what you were talking about, Dana can see him thinking as Dante looks at her with his dark, musing eyes. She can see him trying to trace the tracks of their conversation, how it escalated to love and screaming and Quillan abruptly leaving the house. He's good at puzzles, but she can't tell if Dante will be able to figure this one out.

"It could work," he says eventually, dislodging Dana from her memories of Quillan leaving, Quillan's hurt face, trying so hard to pull a mask over his emotions, failing because he never can, and that's what she hates and loves about him, how he wears his emotions as his own skin and holds his heart in his hands-

"Yes," she says obstinately, "yes, it could."

NINE

Kassia is asleep when Quillan checks on her. She lies curled up on Yeva's threadbare couch, hair splayed across the cushions. Quillan caresses her head tenderly, her red curls soft beneath his hand. Both of the Ks had Grainne's red hair; Quillan's is the color of chocolate and auburn.

Quillan's throat clenches thinking of his mum and sister. He blinks the pain away, trying to ignore the stinging in his eyes.

Bialas is lying on a cot, his injured leg elevated and bandaged. He looks paler than usual, his white hair limp and dull. Quillan will have to keep a close eye on his father. Bialas has always been a bit distant; he's a quiet man, shy and soft-spoken. With Grainne and Klaudia gone now, Quillan is worried about him. When he saw him fleetingly before retiring to Dana's house, Bialas was so far removed from his surroundings. Quillan hadn't stayed long- he was relieved enough just seeing his sister and father, having conformation of their wellbeing- but he had sensed Bialas' detachment.

His Aunt Yeva is puttering around the tiny kitchen trying to pull together some food.

"There's no tea, I'm afraid," she says. "Would you like some tinned tomatoes?"

"No, thanks," Quillan replies softly. He's not feeling hungry.

"You should eat something, Quillan."

He does not reply. Yeva sits down near him, looking at him with concern.

"Did you get your box from Cleophas?"

"What?"

"Cleophas brought your box back with him when he arrived. He was bringing it to the Creares. You were there, weren't you?"

Faintly, Quillan remembers seeing his box on Dana's work table. It hadn't registered to him then.

"Yes," he says, "I was there."

Yeva is not the most intuitive woman, but she's made of common sense and heart. It's quite clear to her that Quillan is being troubled by a multitude of things.

"Come here," she says, standing up, and Quillan obligingly moves into her arms. As she holds him, the tension leaks from Quillan's body and he clings to her, the tears back in his eyes. The choking sensation has returned to his throat and he whimpers, wet pain trickling from his mouth. He cries into his aunt, letting out his demons. Yeva does not speak; there is no need too. Quillan needs this catharsis, and she gives it to him.

The streets are always dim in the Witch Market. The Snitches crave the sun. There are whole generations that have never seen proper sunlight; Quillan's, his father's, the children beneath him. It is a common wish among the Snitches, to see the naked sun. Quillan has dreamed about it before; a gorgeous, raw white light, throwing out shining yellow ribbons.

Quillan walks through the dark, wishing there was more to hear. Usually the Witch Market has a bustle to it; it is a body, every family and individual working together to fulfill the roles of the vital organs and keep the Witch Market alive. Quillan can hear water running, dishes being washed, the thump of cloth, the clap of knives on wood and the snap of cooking meat, the crunch of his boots on the gravel, the crackling of fires and pops of gas stoves- a shudder racks his long frame and he shoves his hands further into his pockets, the pops and cracks reminding him too clearly of the Xs ammunition. Very few people are about; everyone is shut up inside their houses.

He can hear the words and sentences of people through the walls and along the roads, though he does his best to tune their voices out. He doesn't like to eavesdrop, though it really can't be helped. Quillan has always heard extraordinarily well; every sound finds a way to him, many unpleasant. He loves to hear the language of a body most of all, and he remembers Dana and her warm curls and the way her breath hitches and how she swallows. He tenses his shoulders, his walk halted. Dana fades to the rear of his thoughts as he catches sight of a girl at the corner, standing beneath the honey-colored arch of a building.

Stevonna is a young thing, only sixteen, yet the young men and boys of the Witch Market have already come out to chase her feelers. She's pretty; Quillan knows that and she is also aware of the fact. Her face is long and oval, like a foal's, her skin light and gold like the long waves of hair that fall around her face like swathes of cotton. Her pink-checked shirt is faded but clean, and she wears a soft blue skirt and red shoes.

"Hi, Quillan," she says.

Her red mouth is a smile, her lips like the beak of a lily.

"Hi, Stevonna," he responds, and he is taken aback at how leaden his voice sounds.

Stevonna watches him closely with bold blue eyes, so much brighter than the midnight of Dana's.

"You look horrible," she tells him, and the notes of concern in her tone seem to chirp like birdsong. "How are you doing?"

"Badly," he says.

Her lily mouth turns into a sympathetic pout. She is very pretty.

She wraps her skinny arms around him, and Quillan, who thought he wanted to shy away from more hugs and touch, instead feels consoled. Hugging Stevonna is different than hugging his Aunt Yeva, he thinks, his cheek pressed against the top of her shiny blonde head. He closes his eyes, exhaling and feeling a load leave his shoulders. Stevonna is like an elastic young plant, bright and green; he feels unexpectedly safe holding her. The sensation of protecting someone is comforting to him, doubled with the feeling that Stevonna is trying to protect him in return. Her body is slender and warm in his arms. She gives him a squeeze and releases him.

"I heard about your mum and sister. I'm sorry," she tells him, and she truly is.

Quillan bites down on the hot prick in his throat.

"Thank you," he says, his voice like wet paper.

She rubs his arms, looking at him with her blue eyes.

"Do you want to be alone?" she asks.

"I think so," Quillan says, even as he leans into her touch, his heart swelling. He does not want to be alone, not truly. Not ever. But there is a part of him that needs different company, company that is not Stevonna.

"Okay," she says.

She puts a hand on his face and he closes his eyes for a moment, wanting to roll into her touch. Then the hand leaves.

"I'll see you later, Quillan."

"Bye," he says softly as she walks away, red shoes leaving tiny imprints on the gravel.

Quillan sees Cleophas sitting in front of the south door when he leaves the confined roads of the Witch Market. His arms are stacked on his knees, his back pressed against the metal as he looks up at the Witch Market's dark ceiling.

"How long have you been here?" Quillan asks.

"I don't know," Cleophas says. "What time is it?"

Quillan had forgotten how his voice sounds in the rush of all that has occurred this morning. Cleophas always sounds quiet and calm, like the flap of drying linens. There is an old wisdom in his voice, and sometimes Quillan has to remind himself that he is the older of the cousins.

"About ten forty-five, I think."

"Funny," Cleophas murmurs, his eyes still caught in the ceiling. "It seemed so much shorter than that."

He's been there for hours. Quillan is quick to deduce that.

"Are you all right?" Cleophas says suddenly, looking at him.

He looks like a mess, Quillan thinks. Cleophas's fair hair has dust and grit in it, and his face looks hollow. The concern in his voice does not have the same ring as Stevonna's. It wholly takes over his tone, channeling all of his attention directly to Quillan.

"No," he says, and he sounds so tired, so incredibly tired. "Will you walk with me?"

"Of course," Cleophas says, his consonants tender.

Quillan takes his hand and pulls him up and they walk together around the Witch Market.

"You went Up, didn't you?" Quillan says.

"Yes." Cleophas replies simply.

Quillan is quiet as they walk, their steps long and slow. He has often wondered about the lives of the Boxians above them, how they differ so extremely, but he has never dared to venture Up to see them for himself. That has always been Cleophas, but for Cleophas it is not a dare but a draw. He has such a childlike wonder about the world and Quillan learned long ago he cannot keep him in one place. He can't help but be protective of him. He's more a younger brother than a cousin.

"Thank you for bringing them back," he says.

Cleophas just dips his head almost imperceptibly.

"And for my box."

"I thought you'd want it," he says, "How's Dana?"

This is what Quillan has wanted to talk about. He is silent for a long time, and Cleophas echoes him, maintaining a steady muteness as they walk. Quillan knows he will not speak, will not prod him until he begins to talk. Even then, when Quillan spills his heart and frustrations, he will not interrupt or comment. He has already reduced himself entirely to a listener.

"She wants to leave the Witch Market," Quillan starts, "or rather, she wants to move it. Pick it up and put it down somewhere else."

Cleophas says nothing, and Quillan continues.

"I can't see it being done. There's no way to safely move everyone out; people are bound to be killed. She says that'll happen if we stay here anyway, and she's right, to a degree. It does happen. But at least we can protect ourselves while we're inside the Witch Market. We can't do that on the run.

"We don't have anywhere to go either. We'd need to send people out ahead to scout for locations, and how long would that take? How much time and energy would we waste preparing to move if they were killed or never came back and we never knew?

"Even if we did find a place to go, moving everyone would be nearly impossible. There are all the elderly, the children and the pregnant women, and we don't have the means to securely transport them, not to mention all of our belongings. This is our home."

"What if there was an easier way?" Cleophas says.

"If there was an easier way, then yes, I'd be all for it," Quillan says. "But there isn't. It's not even so much the difficulty that upsets me; it's how unsafe it all is. Dana won't hear anything else- you know what she's like. We had a fight."

Cleophas says nothing, waiting.

"I love her," Quillan says, "I love her and yet sometimes the things she does, the things she says— she's so reckless. It's not that she's stupid, because she's not, not at all. It's like she's aware of the danger of the situation and just grabs ahold of it without a single whim. I worry that she's going to hurt herself again."

Dana is a chemist, hence the menagerie of equipment that fills her room. She likes to make explosions, small bombs and grenades. Six years ago, when she was thirteen, one of her experiments went wrong and she blasted away half of her room, earning her acid scars up the length of her right leg and mangling her foot entirely. Though she has walked with a crutch ever since, the incident has never deterred her from her work. Quillan knows she is more than capable of taking care of herself, but he worries that she needs someone to keep an eye on her, to make sure she doesn't take her impassioned actions too far. She is a danger to herself, though she will never acknowledge it.

Quillan has loved her ever since they were children. He

kissed her when they were ten; it took her three years to return the gesture. It is not that Dana is cold; she just does not show her romantic feelings outright.

"I love her," Quillan says, "and I'm worried about her. I understand where she comes from, why she wants to move. Our lives here are horrible. We're nothing. We lose more Snitches each year —"

He chokes on his words, wetness seeping into his tone, and fights to compose himself.

"I don't want to lose her, Cleophas. I can't lose her, not after today. Her idea puts everyone in the Witch Market in danger, and I can't do that. I have to take care of Kassia and my father, and I can't afford to lose anyone else. I just can't."

"I know."

That's all Cleophas has to say. Quillan likes that he can just talk to him, sometimes nearly incessantly, knowing that Cleophas is listening to every word, thinking it over.

"Penny for your thoughts," Quillan says a while later as they walk in and out of the shadows.

"I want to go find Blathnat," Cleophas says.

"The doors are closed, Cleophas, you can't go out."

"There are other ways."

"You shouldn't," Quillan says, with a slight air of reproach. He knows he can't stop him, no matter what he says.

"I know," Cleophas replies, and there is that twinge in his voice that Quillan knows means he feels badly. "But I have to. I know she's all right, but I have to see her."

"All right. Do you want me to come with you?"

"If you want. But I'll be fine."

"I know, just be careful. Please."

"I will."

They have reached a rock fall that cascades down from the dark ceiling, petrified amongst metal and concrete. Cleophas begins to climb it with skill, moving from boulder to boulder, looking like a gargoyle in his black coat. Quillan watches until he disappears through a needle-thin gap high in the rock, vanishing like a shadow in light.

Blathnat

TEN

Moving through the rock fall is always slow work. Age and lack of exposure to the elements cement the rocks in place; they do not shift or creak as they would in nature. Cleophas found a way through them when he was nine. This is his route. Quillan, Dana, and Blathnat know it exists, but Cleophas is the only one who uses it. The passages are slim, some spaces not even a foot wide, and more than once, Cleophas has to suck in his already lithe figure to squeeze through. Often, the passage is more vertical than horizontal, and he climbs like a spider, wedged between the rocks. The space is pitch-black, and Cleophas makes his way by touch and memory.

While Quillan had spoken about his feelings towards Dana, Cleophas could not help but think of Blathnat. While Quillan and Dana have known each other since they were children, Blathnat entered Cleophas's life only a few years ago, and it was only recently that she became such an installation. Initially, she was a friend of Helminette.

Cleophas remembers the first time he saw her. The pair of them had been sitting cross-legged outside of the Ektoses' tent; Blathnat was stringing pink beads into Helminette's hair. Cleophas had not thought much of her at first- she was just another face that he had not seen before- but then he grew curious, as he always does. He began to want to know more about this mysterious girl, and it struck him how truly mysterious she was. He knew nothing about Blathnat. Her story was absent, she never spoke about it. Curiosity started a fire in Cleophas, and he yearned to fuse his life with this girl's, to align their timelines and compare their histories, open their minds together and see how symmetrical they were. He wanted to open her like a pomegranate; break the tough shell and wrap his hands in her jewels, treasuring each individual facet of her.

She was eighteen when he met her, four years his senior, and over the three years that they have interacted, Cleophas has been entrusted with more knowledge about Blathnat Isodle Seren than any other human being. He knows how radiant a creature she is, how unrestrained and enigmatic and alive. He knows her father was in love with her mother's sister, and that both of her parents died when she was a child. He knows she loves to dance, that she can run quickly, and that she loves strawberries more than any other fruit, but she also likes warm corn and pumpkin muffins. She can speak

Welsh and Gaelic as well as English, but she is illiterate in all three, though she desperately wants to learn to read and write. She is playful and coy and Cleophas loves her sense of humor.

When Cleophas was fifteen, Blathnat came to the Ektoses' tent looking for Helminette. Helminette had been out, presumably with her boyfriend, Redman, and Blathnat's soft, golden eyes had turned to Cleophas in her stead. That day, they clicked like puzzle pieces, and Cleophas has never let go of her since. Blathnat's visits are for Cleophas now, not Helminette, and instead of stringing beads in his hair, she holds his hand and takes him to Lower City and old Boston and they spend hours walking or lying still on their backs on rooftops. Sometimes they speak incessantly, diving together into whatever topic comes across their tongues, and sometimes a companionable silence fills the space between them like warm milk. It was during one of these times that Blathnat told him she can hear the stars through the smog. Cleophas has never felt so complete with another person.

He sees less of Blathnat these days. The kiss in the Witch Market was a chance encounter; it is unusual to see her there. She spends most of her time in the city, flitting back and forth from Upper to Lower, never staying anywhere very long. Half the time when Cleophas ventures Up, he keeps an eye out for her, wondering where she is.

She likes sex, Blathnat. Cleophas knows this. She told him once that sometimes she sleeps with people for favors- food, money, trinkets. She had been worried when she told him, worried that such frivolous behavior might end their friendship, but Cleophas had told her honestly that it did not matter to him how many people she slept with, that he would always care about her. Blathnat was grateful.

He does not worry about her often, but he can do nothing to prevent the underlying thread of concern from wrapping itself around him when he sees nothing of Blathnat for weeks. He knows she can take care of herself, and he trusts her better judgment, but Cleophas has a big heart, and his concern is like a second skin that he cannot be rid of. His want to see her has swollen, and Cleophas wants to see her so badly, to kiss her and press his cheek against her chest and tell her everything. He loves her, and he wants her to know it as much as he does so that when they are apart, love at least, will connect them.

As he reaches the end of the convoluted passage, watery light seeps over the rocks like melted silver. The space widens marginally, until Cleophas is pushing himself out of the rocks like a blind thing thrust into the sun. He emerges in a rundown part of Lower City, a dark, dreary area behind a row of stinking cafés and twenty-four hour convenience stores. He must be as inconspicuous as possible. In Upper

City, it is easy for him to blend in among the air traffic on his hoverbike; he can move quickly enough to be unnoticeable and his black coat and general visage do not attract attention. In Lower City, people are far more prone to ask questions if he's not careful, and Cleophas does not have his hoverbike to escape on if the law decides to hound him.

He turns onto the street and walks quickly, his steps soft as he hugs the shadows, wearing the darkness like a second jacket. He crosses his arms, reinstating his olfactory walls. His sensory guard had been let down in the rock fall, but now the scent of stone is gone, and hundreds of others come to flood his senses. The smell of bad coffee leaks from the cafés, and he knows most of them opened early, as evident by the smell of cinnamon and burnt sugar wafting from the rear of the bakeries. The convenience stores reek of oil and gasoline. Several people loiter outside the doors smoking cigarettes that smell like roses; the latest fad in Lower City.

He sees a woman with blue hair and for a moment the palpitations of his heart increase, but her hair is tied in knot above her head and her face is round. She has none of Blathnat's beauty.

At the end of the street, the silver clad body of a police officer appears. Cleophas moves discretely behind the nearest building, pressing his back against the wall and not daring even to breathe. He does not move until the officer passes by the sour-smelling bakery; then he closes his eyes for a long breath, tension unraveling from his body. When he opens his eyes, he notices a long pink coat trailing from the fire escape of the building adjacent to the bakery. Blue hair drapes over the collar, long and damaged by dye.

"Blathnat?" Cleophas whispers, and though there is no way she can hear him, she turns and looks down.

"Cleophas," she exclaims, and she descends the fire escape in a flurry of limbs, pink coat billowing out like a sail. She flings her arms around him when she reaches him, hoisting him in the air and holding him to her as he loops his arms around her neck. They clutch each other tightly, Cleophas's legs cinched around her sides. When she puts him down, her hands move to his face and she kisses him a hundred times, enveloping his lips over and over as she kisses him quickly and repeatedly. Her hands frame his face like the covers of a book.

Hello, I love you, how are you, what happened, I'm so glad to see you, I love you, I love you.

Eventually the kisses slow the way rain does as it reaches its end. The touches of their lips become tender and long, and Cleophas's mouth opens up like a rose beneath Blathnat's. He is reminded of a poem he read long ago.

"I love you," he tells her, his words like unrolled parchment. "I'm in love with you."

"I know," she says softly, and he closes his eyes as her smell soaks him, as her voice wraps him up like a package in brown silk. "I love you, too."

"I know about the extermination," she says as they sit together on the fire escape, hands clasped together like a single seashell.

Cleophas nods.

"I was Up."

"So was I. I was watching the celebrations. I wanted to go find you as soon as I found out, but the doors were closed. I saw the ashes though," she says, growing quieter. "There were so many."

Cleophas can only nod again. He does not speak and Blathnat does not ask him to. She knows he will tell her when he's ready.

"They killed Mum," he says. "My dad's hurt; he got shot. They got Aunt Grainne too, and Klaudia. Quillan's coping, but it's difficult for him. His father is so distant."

"What about you? Are you coping?"

Cleophas looks down at their conjoined hands, at his dirty, bandaged fingers and Blathnat's long, white ones.

"It doesn't seem real," he says, choking up. "I saw one of the Xs kill a little boy on my way back to the Witch Market, and that feels real, because I know. I saw. But with Mum and

Aunt Grainne and Klaudia, I can almost pretend they're still alive. I just keep thinking about the last time I saw them. I wish I could have said goodbye to them. I didn't get to have any closure and now my memory of them feels so incomplete. Not even the ashes seemed like them. They didn't smell like them. They didn't smell at all."

The shadows settle around them while they sit, rolling over the silence like black phantoms. Though the light is grimy and thin, it is still brighter up here than anywhere in old Boston. Cleophas watches a spider on the fire escape, observing the jerky, marionette-like movements of its legs. The fluffy cuff of Blathnat's coat is brushing against his skin.

"Where did you get this?" he asks, picking at the fabric with his fingers.

The coat is floor length, soft and warm. Its toggles are unemployed, leaving it flopping open, and the cuffs and collar are both lined with feathery, synthetic pink fur. Cleophas has never seen it before.

"Salamasina gave it to me," Blathnat says. "She said it isn't her color. I'm not sure it's mine either, but it's comfortable."

Cleophas lays his head on her shoulder in response. Salamasina is one of Blathnat's dancer friends. Cleophas has met her once; she's a strikingly gorgeous woman, all curves and caramel skin and a river of black hair as thick as tar.

"Dana wants to move the Witch Market," he says quietly.

crumpled paper bags. There is the squeak of a hinge and the backdoor opens. A thin man wearing an apron appears, a plastic bag of trash in his hand. Alarm lights his face at the sight of the two of them and he stutters to speak.

"Please, my friend hasn't eaten in four days," Blathnat says, cutting him off and doubling the number Cleophas gave her. "Can you spare anything?"

The man shuts his mouth. His shock is fading, and Cleophas can see him thinking. He studies the pair of them for long minutes, his gaze scrutinizing, looking at Blathnat's pink coat and the string of beads in her hair and Cleophas's small frame and bandaged hands.

"Fine," he grunts eventually. "Wait here."

He dumps the trash in the bin and heads inside, shutting the door behind him. About a minute later he returns, a brown paper bag clutched in his fist. Blathnat takes it.

"Thank you," she says.

The man says nothing and Cleophas feels a knot form in his belly.

"You're Snitches, aren't you?" he says, and the knot grows and tightens sickeningly around Cleophas's stomach. Blathnat says nothing, her large golden eyes fixed unblinkingly on the baker's muddy brown ones.

"The Xs were out this morning," he says. "They were going on an extermination. But they clearly didn't get all of you, huh?"

Fear has frozen over Cleophas like a shell of ice. He reaches for Blathnat's hand, fingers wrapping around the fluffy cuff of her sleeve. The baker's eyes fixate on the movement, and he looks at the two of them again.

"Go. Get out of here. Don't come here again!" he tells them gruffly, and shuts the door.

In the bag are two chocolate doughnuts. The bottoms are black and crusty. Cleophas scrapes the burnt part off before eating his, savoring each crumb. The sweetness bursts in his mouth. He hasn't tasted chocolate in over a year. When they have both finished, they sit out of sight against the rocks that hide the sliver-sized entrance to the Witch Market.

"Will you come back with me?" Cleophas asks.

"I can't," Blathnat says, and Cleophas wishes he could bury himself in the velvet of her voice.

"Why?" he asks, aware of how much he sounds like a child.

"I have an appointment later. And anyway," she kisses the top of his head, "I'm taller than you; you know I wouldn't fit."

"What kind of appointment do you have?" he asks.

"It's just a lesson," Blathnat replies, trying to downplay the statement with a shrug. "I'm learning how to read and write."

"In English?"

She nods.

"I can teach you that," Cleophas says softly, feeling like a rejected animal.

"I know you could, but I don't get to see you often." she says consolingly. "These lessons are going to be very consistent."

"You could always spend more time in the Witch Market."

"They don't like me, Cleophas, not the way you do."

"No one likes you like I do." he says, looking over into her golden eyes.

"I know that." she whispers, opening her mouth and kissing him.

But Blathnat is right. She is not well thought of or even well known among the Snitches. She is unknown because she spends so little time in the Witch Market, and those that do know her are judgmental of the quantity of time she spends Up, frolicking with the Boxians.

"I have to go," Cleophas whispers, his words like butterflies on Blathnat's skin. "They'll notice I'm gone."

"Then go," she says. "I'll see you later."

"When?"

The question is delivered like an open rose.

"I don't know, Cleophas. But I will see you."

"I love you, Blathnat."

"I love you, Cleophas."

Their lips meld together like the pages of one book. Cleophas can taste the chocolate in her mouth. Once again, he is reminded of a poem.

ELEVEN

Fontaine sits at the kitchen table, musing in silence. Finally, he says, "I think we could do it."

Dana leans forward, an eager light in her eyes.

"Go on," she says.

"We'd have to send some sort of search party out, of course," Fontaine says. "But that shouldn't be too hard to do. Once we have a set location in mind, everything becomes more visible. It's a solid idea, Dana. As long as you take small steps in the beginning, I don't see why we can't move the Witch Market. The only trouble you'll have getting this thing in the air is convincing everyone it's our only option for survival."

Dana's eyes glint.

"That's where I need you."

Her brother's eyebrows rise.

"How so?" he asks.

"People like you, Fontaine," Dana says, "you're intelligent, you're good-looking, you get around; people know who you are, they listen when you talk. I'm a grump who blows things up."

"I'm not going to pitch this for you, Dana," Fontaine says with a wry expression.

Dana opens her mouth to retort, but he continues, cutting her off.

"Dana, you're an excellent speaker. More than anything, you exude passion when you talk. Well, that or a dry disinterest, but that's not relevant here. You want this. I'll help you as much as I can; you already have me hooked. I want to leave. But you're the driving force behind this. It's your idea. You have to be the one to deliver it."

Dana is quiet for a while. Out of the blue, she wishes they had more wine in the house.

"All right," she says, "I'll do it."

"Good," Fontaine says, getting to his feet. "I've got you on this one."

"Where are you going?" she asks, watching him pick his way across the clutter of the main room.

"To see Rainart." he replies.

"You two spending the day together?"

"Perhaps. Maybe more than the day."

"Give him a kiss for me, then," she says, thinly veiled amusement dousing her.

"I just might."

"Get out of here," she says, waving her hand and grinning. "Oh, Fontaine, can you bring some bottles back with you? Dad and I emptied the last of the white earlier."

"You hate white wine."

"I know, but Dad likes it, I needed a drink, and we were out of red. Just get a few bottles of each."

"Where is Dad?"

"At the Archive. He said something about getting a copy of *Frankenstein*."

"He can't be done with *War and Peace* yet, he just picked that up a few days ago."

He's not; you know how he is, he likes to change it up."

Fontaine hasn't been gone two minutes before he appears again, hanging around the door.

"Hey, Dana, when do you want to have a meeting about this? Moving the Witch Market, I mean."

"As soon as possible," she says. "Tonight, if the news can travel enough."

"How about ten at the Archive? The space is big enough, and that's enough time for word to get around. The extermination shock will have worn off some by then as well."

"All right."

"I'll tell Rainart about it, I'm sure he'll be interested."

Dana nods and Fontaine leaves. Silence swirls around her

in the thick, yellowy lamplight as she sits at the table. She extends her right leg gingerly, exhaling as she stretches the muscles of the injured flesh. Her mouth feels dry, and excitement laces her body like vines of electricity.

This will work. We will move the Witch Market.

The Archive is the largest building in the Witch Market. It was once a grocery store of sorts, but any defining features have since been worn down to nothing. The Archive is the library of the Snitches, the largest conglomeration of information in the Witch Market. From the floor rise towers of crates and boxes loaded with books, creating a forest of columns to weave between. Open file cabinets dot the space in between like mushrooms, storing scans and tablets pressed together like playing cards. Great paintings and prints hang and lean on the walls, pieces of old artwork that have been saved from the decomposition of age. Each Snitch has their own personal possessions they keep in their house or tent, but the Archive belongs to everyone. It is the greatest treasure of the Snitches. Its words and stories and secrets are what fuels them above any food or drink. The Snitches are guardians, preservers of the old words. Without the Archive, they would have nothing.

Dana arrives at nine p.m., walking crookedly between the columns. People move like moths in the Archive, flickering in and out of the shadows and gathering around lamps to read by the brown and gold light. She hears their whispers as she walks by, feels the glances like feathery touches; the news has spread. *Thank you, Fontaine.*

A familiar figure is sitting in a circle of papers and scans, pouring over a tablet. Dana limps over and eases herself down across from him.

"Hi, Cleophas," she says.

Cleophas's blonde head jerks up, and he launches himself across the papers, wrapping his arms around Dana.

"Dana!" he exclaims, and she feels warmer as he hugs her. He reminds her so much of a little boy sometimes.

"How are you?" he asks, speaking into her hair.

"I'm fine," she says, the corner of her mouth twitching into a smile. "How are you doing?"

"Okay," he says quietly, and she knows he is thinking about his mother. "We're alive. That matters."

"Yes," she agrees, as he unwraps himself from around her and sits back. "That matters. What are you doing?" she asks, looking at the papers scattered across the floor.

Cleophas looks forlornly at the mess.

"I was looking for a poem," he says.

"Why?"

"It's for Blathnat." He blushes.

The color in his cheeks makes Dana smile. She loves this

boy so much. He's like a younger brother to her.

"What's the poem?"

"I don't know," Cleophas explains, the forlorn look coming back to his face. "I can only remember a bit of it. It's E.E. Cummings, I think; the style is somewhat jilted."

"What's the part you remember?"

Cleophas's grey eyes gaze toward the ceiling as he concentrates.

"I do not know what it is about you that closes and opens; only something in me understands the voice of your eyes is deeper than all roses. Nobody, not even the rain, has such small hands."

"It's lovely," Dana says, and the blush returns to Cleophas's cheeks.

"There's a lot of opening and unclosing," he says, "I just can't remember the title, so I've been reading through poems, trying to find it."

"Have you found E.E. Cummings yet?"

"No, I got distracted by Keats and Kramarik," he says sheepishly.

"They're filed alphabetically —"

"By author, yes; I realized it was by Cummings after I started looking. And I've made a bit of a mess."

He trails off, looking over the small river of papers and plastic scans. Dana helps him shift through the poetry, ordering them into piles, occasionally looking over a line of verse.

"Here it is," Cleophas says excitedly, "*somewhere i have never traveled,gladly beyond.* I knew I wouldn't remember the title, but it has the same bits."

"Read it to me."

"*somewhere i have never traveled,gladly beyond*
By e.e. cummings

"*somewhere I have never traveled, gladly beyond*
any experience, your eyes have their silence:
in your most frail gesture are things which enclose me,
or which I cannot touch because they are too near

"*your slightest look easily will unclose me*
though I have closed myself as fingers,
you open always petal by petal myself as Spring opens
(touching skillfully, mysteriously) her first rose

"*or if your wish be to close me, I and*
my life will shut very beautifully, suddenly,
as when the heart of this flower imagines
the snow carefully everywhere descending;

"*nothing which we are to perceive in this world equals*

the power of your intense fragility: whose texture
compels me with the color of its countries,
rendering death and forever with each breathing

"(I do not know what it is about you that closes
and opens; only something in me understands
the voice of your eyes is deeper than all roses)
nobody, not even the rain, has such small hands"

"That's lovely," Dana says. "Will you give it to her?"

Cleophas nods.

"I think so."

He folds the poem up carefully, tucking it away in his coat.

"Dana," he says softly, as they pack the poems back into the boxes, "people are watching you."

"I know," she says. She can feel the eyes on her like marbles dripping down her spine. The number of people in the Archive has swelled considerably. They walk about like shadows, moving in groups and whispering.

"It's about the move, isn't it?" Cleophas says, voice still hushed, "Moving the Witch Market. Quillan told me."

"Yes," Dana replies. She looks at him sharply over a sheaf of poems. "Are you in? Will you go with us?"

"Yes."

"Do you think I can do it, Cleophas? Do you think I can

convince them?"

Cleophas is the only person Dana feels comfortable opening up to like this. She has always found his faith in her to be more reassuring than anyone else's. Dana lives on top of high walls; it is not often that she leaves them, but she leaves them for Cleophas.

"I do," Cleophas tells her, gray eyes looking into her blue ones. "I think you can do anything you set your mind to."Dante appears over the two of them, his figure casting them in darkness.

"Good evening, Cleophas," he says, extending a hand and helping him up. His dark eyes are full of mystery as he looks at Dana.

"We're all ready for you," he says, and there is pride woven among the palette of his words.

"It's early," she points out.

"It is. But we've always made our own time."

Dana sits at the large circular table in the center of the Archive. Cleophas curls up by her feet like a cat beneath the table. Snitches have gathered in orbital hoops around it, watching those present and waiting. Dante and Fontaine take seats on either side of Dana. She casts strong looks around the table at the others present. Most prominent is Neckarios, whose daughter is that mischievous flirt of a girl, Stevonna. Dana thinks Neckarios looks like a lion. He is a slender man with a thick golden beard and hair that reaches his shoulders. Wealth in the Witch Market is measured by material possession and influence, and Neckarios has a lot of both. While the Creares are high in that regard as well, Dana will have to gain Neckarios's support to win over the more reluctant Snitches.

Her Uncle Twyford sits directly across from her with his boyfriend Ferenc. Twyford will be an easy sell. His green eyes are already glittering with excitement, his mouth in that familiar, lopsided grin he wears perpetually. Twyford is a magnet. He's sexy and social and talkative and is very well-liked. Dana can already tell that he will agree to go with her.

Also at the table is the doctor, Leon; Cleophas's great Uncle Nicodemus; Quillan's Aunt Lichah; the couple Muga and Godfreya; Regan; and Iris. Dana analyzes them each. Muga and Godfreya are quiet, both wives calmly waiting for the proceedings to begin. They will agree to go as long as Dana's pitch sounds reasonable and neither will interrupt her. Lichah will also respect her speech, but she will prod and poke until she gets the understanding she wants. Regan and Leon are both wildcards. Regan is controlled by his wife, Ivonne; Dana is not surprised to see her standing behind him, her face stormy. It was their son who was gunned down by the Xs when Cleophas returned to the Witch Market. Dana does not know which way they will turn. The same is true of

Leon. Dana has never been able to read the doctor's thoughts or emotions. He wears an indifferent mask. If she can sell the move to the doctor, then her job will become much easier. Grand Nic's body language is just as impassive, but there is a light in his eyes, a curiosity that Dana will do well to keep.

From beneath the table, Cleophas says, "The city has fifty million citizens. It's a maxia now."

"You went Up?" Dana whispers to him.

He nods.

"You're not angry with me," he says, surprised.

"Not today," she says.

Across the table, Neckarios clears his throat and all eyes turn toward him.

"I think we're all aware of the rumors that have been circulating within the Witch Market today," he says. "Well, we're here now. Dante, care to explain the meaning of this?"

"You're addressing the wrong person, Neckarios," Dante replies. "I have no part in this matter other than to offer my support. Any questions you have should be directed to Dana."

Neckarios's expression changes and he runs a hand through his blonde hair in an attempt to hide his surprise. Dana does not miss it.

"Well then, Dana," he says. "What do you have to say about this?"

Dana

TWELVE

Dana takes a moment, looking past Neckarios at the rings of Snitches gathered around the table, watching and waiting.

"I can only imagine how distorted the whispers have become over the past hours," she says, "So I'll begin by clarifying my proposal, to avoid any further confusion.

"We've been here, hiding underneath Boston, for almost sixty years, ever since the Culture Wipe. Generations of us have grown up here, born without ever seeing the sky, or the stars, or proper sunlight. Our knowledge of these things comes from our grandparents and great grandparents, our elders who have seen these things with their own eyes. We cling to memories that are not even our own, and we're losing them to pictures and scans and stories. We're preserving what we have never personally experienced.

"Each year we take a gamble with the new lives we have to care for, the people that are our responsibility —"

It is now that she sees Quillan, standing in the ochre shadows of the rings, all chocolate and auburn and autumn. If he were a season, he would be fall. He's standing next to that girl, Stevonna. Her blonde hair matches her father's. Quillan's face is dark. Dana looks away from him, picking up her place.

"We never know if we will have enough food to last us the year. We aren't allowed to think about the future; it's too precarious an idea. Yes, we have the hothouse- it's precious to us all- but it is a slender thread down here. When the ripening comes, we're happy and we're fed, but it's such a short time, and there is never truly enough to go around. So we resort to stealing. We become the very things the Boxians see us as, because it is the only way we know to survive. We put ourselves at risk to sneak Up and steal- but we never take much, because we're so terrified of being caught. We never know when we may have to shut off our link to the water supply, and each year when our holes are repaired, we have to drill our way through stronger reinforcements.

"We live our whole lives in struggle and fear. We never know when the Xs will arrive with their weapons and their bullets, killing the Snitches who live outside the doors only as a last resort, jeopardizing their safety because they find the confines of the Witch Market too claustrophobic. We've seen what happens to them too many times. The Xs kill our mothers and fathers, our sisters and brothers, sons and daughters. They kill our grandparents and our children, our history and our future. And we let them, because there is nothing we believe we can do. We are struggling to survive, to get through each day, each month, each year.

"I don't want to survive," she says, looking levelly around the table. "I want to live. I want to be able to see the sun for myself. I want to walk with grass under my feet, not pavement or rock or concrete. I want to live in a proper house, not a hut or a tent or a home built of scrap and metal. I want a life without fear to be a reality, not a dream. This is why I want to leave the Witch Market."

There are stirrings in the rings, but no one seems very surprised by the statement. The rumors have said that much.

"It's a very pretty speech," a voice says, and Dana sees Speero among the crowd. She bites back an exasperated snort. She finds Speero repugnant; he's nineteen, only a year older than her, and she despises everything about him, from his snide voice to the scrubby black facial hair he wears on his chin. She can see his growing discomfort as no one steps in to speak, and wants to smirk as he scrambles for words.

"But, do you think it's possible?"

A weak retort.

"Yes," Dana says.

"I think what Speero is trying to express is the doubt of such a thing actually coming to pass," Neckarios says, coming to his rescue. "We can't just *leave* the Witch Market. It's a wonderful thought, but isn't it just as you said yourself? A dream?"

"A dream that is becoming real," Dana says firmly. "It's a dream as long as we think it's a dream, but the minute we choose to act, that dream grows legs. We've been here so long that we've even forgotten about building castles in the air. This is my castle, and all we have to do is start laying foundations, and it will be attainable. Why should we stay here? It has never done us any good."

"We avoided the Culture Wipe," Leon points out.

"Yes, that's true," Dana acknowledges with a nod, "But that doesn't help the fact that we will ultimately waste away, and when we do, the Witch Market will have been nothing against the Culture Wipe. We don't have to leave our lives behind. We're just leaving the fear, the insecurity that our lives are ridden with."

"We do not know what the fate of the Witch Market will be," Neckarios counters. "It is no fact that we will "waste away", as you put it."

"The Xs will find a way into the Witch Market eventually," Dana says, "We hide here because the doors protect us, but how long will that last?"

"The Xs never pursue us past the fences —"

"That they melt and crush to the ground. The extermination this morning was one of the largest we've ever experienced. We lost over a hundred people living outside the Witch Market. How many were wounded?"

"Sixty," Leon supplies.

"There you have it," Dana says. "The Xs pursued us further than ever before today. They know about the south door."

"But they will never be able to get through it," Neckarios says confidently, despite the anxious murmurs in the crowd around them.

"They are *learning*," Dana stresses, fighting to drive home her point, "Who is to say they will stop, now that they know where we mass together? They may act like machines, and I think we forget that they are not, that the Xs are *people*, and smart people. Their technology is greater than ours. They will find a way through eventually, and then what will we do? Cower like trapped mice in a cage of our own making."

"As opposed to stepping willingly into the slaughterhouse in a brash attempt to escape?" Neckarios says. "I see no difference between the two."

"Well, I don't know about you, but I would rather have a choice in the matter of my death," Dana says.

There are titters among the rings of Snitches at her words. Dana works to compose herself, clasping her hands together on the table. Neckarios clears his throat again, eyes fluttering about the table.

"So, hypothetically speaking, if we were to do this move,

how would we transport the Archive? We can't just leave it behind."

It is an empty attempt to shift the focus, and skepticism still riddles his voice. Dana pauses before she speaks. She must choose her words carefully. Dana does not have the same attachment to legends and heritage that most of the Snitches share. Unlike her father, she is not a packrat and does not care for material things. Dana is a creature of science and mechanics. She destroys; she does not preserve or create. She must find ways to accommodate the rest of the Snitches in this regard; if her plan does not include a future for the Archive, then her support will be minimal, if any at all.

"Of course the Archive will come with us, but it will be an arduous process." Dana begins, "I must stress that my immediate priorities are the safety of our lives first, and the Archive second. That said, I think we can move the Archive the same way we would move ourselves: by using the grocery vans."

"What grocery vans?" Lichah asks.

"The same ones that we take our food from," Dana replies, "I don't imagine it would be difficult to hijack a few of them; after all, we steal from them all the time."

"Why, that's preposterous," Neckarios says. "It's fine for us to take from the vans; we need to in order to survive. But we can't possibly —"

"We know all that we need to know to take them," Dana says, cutting him off. "We know their cycles, when they arrive and leave and how much time there is in between. We know their carrying capacity and the routes that they frequent and the ones that are used less. We know that they are seldom guarded, and when they are the defenses are weak. It is entirely plausible that we could take the vans and use them for safe transport. No one blinks an eye at supply vans. We would be invisible."

"It risks the lives of our people," Neckarios says.

"Lives are risked whenever someone goes Up," Dana protests, her irritation growing stronger. "The only difference is what you attach to them. There will always be danger when we go Up, but this is something we need and we are capable of taking it. The only thing holding us back is fear, and the only reason that fear is stronger now is because you don't know if the outcome will be good. But we can't know all of these things for certain. We can know a lot, but we have to take a leap of faith at some point, otherwise we'll never get off the ground."

Silence follows her words, and Dana can feel the energy vibrating in the Archive. She keeps her gaze focused on Neckarios, and feels others begin to do the same. His word, his influence, will dictate whether or not the Witch Market goes. Dana can see him growing squeamish under the scrutinizing looks of the Snitches, and he clears his throat abruptly. He lays his clasped hands on the table before him.

"Well then," he says, "continue."

Relief rolls off Dana's shoulders like a wave, worry and anxiety receding like an old tide. Grand Nicodemus raises a hand slightly.

"If I may," he says, and Dana nods to him.

"I am wondering where it is we will go."

"I thought New Hampshire," Dana says.

There is a flurry of words and whispering at this bit of news. Speero speaks out above them.

"Why New Hampshire?"

"Why not?" Dana says. "The border is only an hour from BostonMaxia, and there are many areas where it is not patrolled. The state is almost empty, ever since the rush to the maxias years ago. It has everything we could want and need. Open space, mountains, waterfront. We could have proper lives there, homes and gardens and safety. I do not know a route yet, but I have no doubt we can find one."

There are nods from places around the table and Dana is glad that this is one point she does not have to force.

"Do you have some sort of party in mind?" Muga asks, "A scouting party, to find and secure an area before the whole move?"

"I've thought about that, yes," Dana says.

"I wouldn't think any more than twenty people," Leon chimes in. His words are greeted by more nods and agreeing murmurs.

"Definitely no one under twenty either." Regan says, and there are more murmurs.

"I'll lead it," Iris speaks up, her Indonesian voice delicate and pronounced among the others. She straightens and looks up from the table as all eyes turn towards her. There is sadness on her face, stuck there like wet paper, and she seems to have aged ten years since Tancred's death. Her dark hair is limp and bedraggled, but there is a firm set to her eyes, despite the tiredness there. Dana approves.

"Are you sure you want to do this?" Neckarios asks.

Iris nods solidly. There will be no shaking her stance. Dana feels some sympathy for the woman and her loss, and she is proud of her strength.

"I'll go," a female voice speaks up from the surrounding crowd, and Dana feels Cleophas stir beneath the table. Helminette, his pretty, older sister emerges from the rings, her husband Redman beside her. Their hands are laced tightly together.

"I'm sure we can delegate the makeup of the scouting party in due time," Dante says, and Dana is aware of the tension radiating from Cleophas's form. She tries not to concern herself with his worry, concentrating her attention on the table and the matter at hand.

"That said, I think we've covered just about everything that can be said at this time," Dante continues, "unless you have anything else to add, Dana?"

"No," Dana says, shaking her head slightly.

"All right then," Neckarios says, clearing his throat again. "Anyone interested in being a part of this scouting party can reconvene here tomorrow at noon. I'll be there to supervise."

He looks pointedly at Dana and Dante, who respond in kind.

"Very well," Grand Nicodemus says, "we're done here. Dana, if I could have a word?"

"Of course," Dana replies, trying not to let her surprise show. She stays seated at the table as the rings of Snitches disperse. Cleophas flies out from beneath the table like a bat, and she quickly loses sight of him, though she sees the back of Quillan's head as he leaves. Dante lays a hand on her shoulder before he leaves, giving it a squeeze that communicates all she needs to know. Grand Nicodemus waits until the area around them has emptied before moving his chair closer to Dana's.

"You're a brave young woman," he says quietly, "You're very lucky."

Dana says nothing. Grand Nic fixes her with a penetrating stare that she cannot decipher.

"This isn't over yet," he tells her, and his words resonate deep within Dana's organs. "This is the very beginning of your fight. Neckarios has agreed to go along with your plan, but he still doubts it. More than anything else, he doubts you.

"The people want this. They like your idea. They like to *hope*. It's a new concept for them, and you will have to fight to keep it thriving."

He takes a moment to wallow in the quiet of the Archive, the low light casting deep shadows in the crevices of his face.

"You are right, though," he says, and his voice is barely a whisper. His eyes are like the old pits of the ocean.

"I see it every year. I remember when it began. I'm old."

He takes Dana's hand unexpectedly, and she jerks at the sensation of his firm hand tightening around hers.

"The Xs are gaining ground. At this rate, they will enter the Witch Market before the end of summer. You have a time table, Dana. At this time, the Snitches are not aware of the danger — at least no more than usual. But they need a leader if we are to get out of this alive, as you have encouraged them to hope. You can be that leader, but you must be careful. Don't get too confident."

Dana's mouth feels dry, as though she has eaten a tablespoon of sand. Grand Nicodemus gives her hand a squeeze, tight and hard, so much different from the touch Dante left on her shoulder. Then he lets go of her and leaves her alone at the table, surrounded by brown light and history and the forbidding sense of a sea waiting to break down a dyke.

THIRTEEN

Cleophas feels tiny. Huddled in the folds of his coat with his back pressed against the wall of his sister's house, he berates himself for not having the courage to knock on the door and ask her- *Why?* he thinks, feeling like a petulant child. He followed Helminette and Redman from the Archive as soon as the meeting dispersed, trying to make a plan in his head of what he would say to her, but the words kept running away like cockroaches in light the moment he thought of them. Now, sitting outside her house, nothing seems to make sense anymore.

Cleophas used to be quite close to Helminette. He always admired her, his pretty sister with her long blonde hair and big brown eyes. She had been his protector, his partner in all things fun. When they were younger, Speero used to bully Cleophas and make fun of his sensitive sense of smell, until one day Helminette punched him in the nose. The two of them used to build forts together, often dismantling the tent in the making. Their father would be angry, but his scolds always ended in laughter as he helped them put the tent back in order.

But then Helminette grew old; too old, it seemed, to build forts and play games with Cleophas and listen to their mother's bedtime stories. She stayed out longer, spent less time at home, and brought back exciting, interesting new friends. One day she brought back Blathnat. Cleophas feels a pang of guilt for being so selfish, when it is really due to Helminette that he has such beauty in his life.

When Helminette met Redman, her time spent at home morphed into visits instead of residence. Cleophas saw less and less of her, only heard news of house plans and wedding preparations. Cleophas was happy at her wedding, but he also felt a sick sadness in his stomach the entire day. Helminette stopped being a constant in his life, and now Cleophas feels as though they are two strangers who barely know each other. The last time he spoke to her was days before the extermination. Cleophas shudders at the thought of it, remembering the ruins he walked through this morning. He feels as though he has already lost enough of Helminette. He does not want to lose her anymore.

Cleophas's morals beat inside his head and he rolls his fingers into fists. Helminette is an adult. She can do what she wants with her life, make her own decisions. She has that right. Cleophas wishes they were still children; that way their parents could decide what she would and wouldn't do.

He cringes. What a selfish thing to want.

It's not that he does not want to leave the Witch Market, he thinks, feeling weak and hypocritical. *It's that I don't want her to go.*

It's dangerous.

Going Up is dangerous, he thinks.

She can make her own choices.

I know.

I've already lost Mum.

I know.

Cleophas waits until he can no longer hear his sister and her husband before leaving. His bandaged fingers are cold, and he stuffs them inside his coat pockets, coming across the poem from the Archive. *Somewhere I Have Never Traveled, Gladly Beyond.* Cleophas feels as though he is being reprimanded. Helminette has let go of him, but that does not mean she does not care about him. He must learn to let go of her. They are not children anymore. They are moving off into the world, both of them. Helminette has always been the first of them to try something new. Someone must lead the way for the others to follow.

Stones seem to fall from Cleophas's back as he walks, trying to rid himself of worries. He holds the poem gently, trying to commit the verses to memory. He reads the lines aloud as he walks, whispering them to himself and as he does so, his mind swells with images of Blathnat. The earthy sweetness of her smell, the way she moves as though she is a perpetually dancing plant, the feel of her hair on his face and her fingers twined through his own.

"*I do not know what it is about you that closes and opens,*" he says, the words like paper swans taking flight from his tongue. "*Only something in me understands the voice of your eyes is deeper than all roses. Nobody, not even the rain, has such small hands.*"

He presses the poem against his heart as he walks, layering the words over each other like blankets, weaving them into his memory like silk ribbons and flowers, creating a thrumming tapestry of verse.

The Ektoses' teakettle house is quiet when Cleophas arrives. Gamma and Grand, sitting at the table, end their discussion when he enters to make tea and retire. Gamma sets up a bed for Cleophas on the ratty velvet sofa and runs a hand through his short hair. He curls up on the cushions like a cat, still wrapped in the protective shell of his coat, the shape of the poem on his lips even as he falls asleep.

FOURTEEN

Quillan steers clear of the Creare house the next day, and many days after. He does not go to the Archive for fear of crossing paths with Dana. Most of his time is spent at Yeva's house, looking after Bialas and Kassia. There is a conundrum in where they will stay. Aunt Yeva can hold them temporarily, but there is no room in her home for Quillan to sleep there. He spends his evenings at his Aunt Lichah's house, which causes a problem when Kassia wants him to sleep with her. She has nightmares, and Bialas is too caught up in his own, day and night, to comfort her.

Quillan wants to get out of Lichah's house. He doesn't mind the company of her wife, Ayako, but Lichah's personality is too abrasive to get along with his own. The morning after the first meeting at the Archve, she bombarded him with questions about the nature of his and Dana's relationship and berated his disagreement towards the move. He left as soon as he could, going straight to Aunt Yeva's to check on Kassia. He wants to set up a proper home for the remainder of his family, but he's angry when he realizes that because of the move, any home he builds will be merely a temporary place.

There seems to be nothing concrete in his life anymore. Grainne, who used to be his bedrock, is gone. His father has reverted so far into himself that nothing Quillan can do seems to reach him. Quillan makes sure Bialas eats and drinks and he checks on the mending of his leg, but he cannot pull his father out. He seems completely empty of his former self. Quillan sometimes sees him sweating profusely and shaking, his eyes wide with a terror that festers in his mind, and he has to grab his hands and shoulders and speak to him until he comes free of the state. Quillan does not know what he sees on these occasions, whether he hallucinates or if his head is flooded with terrible memories. He is not sure he wants to know.

One day, when Bialas has fallen asleep after another episode, Yeva tells Quillan a story.

"When we were kids, your dad had a twin sister."

Quillan knows this.

"I know she died," he says, "but I don't know how."

"Basha was killed in an extermination," Aunt Yeva explains, "It was one of the largest the Witch Market has ever seen. Everyone lost someone. It took years for people to have the courage to go back out beyond the doors.

"Basha and Bialas were inseparable. He was much different as a child; curious, inquisitive to the point of annoyance, incredibly talkative. He changed after Basha died. They were eight then. Bialas retreated from the world; he seldom spoke and nothing could excite him. When Grainne entered the picture, he opened up. Slowly, his personality metamorphosed again. He loved your mother very much, you know."

Quillan nods tightly, a slight jerk of his jaw. He looks at his father, asleep on the couch. His hair, white since birth, is brushed back from his face; he looks almost peaceful, but Quillan cannot tell if he dreams or not.

The days pass quickly. Quillan hears the news secondhand; how the scouting party is formed, what route they will be taking, how they will communicate with the others at the Witch Market. It will only take an hour to get over the border, they say, and then two weeks will be allotted to find a location. After that time, and if there is no communication, the worst will be assumed and the move abandoned. Stevonna tells him most of this. She hangs around him a lot, entertaining Kassia, touching. She likes to touch, Quillan has noticed. Her hands brush along his arms and back as she passes him. They find his shoulders when he sits down, squeezing and massaging the crooks in his neck.

Today they are in one of the common areas, a sort of junkyard of furniture and relics too threadbare and damaged for anyone to want. Quillan is stretched out on a lumpy sofa, his head in Stevonna's lap. Kassia is nearby, playing a game with some other nine year-olds. He can hear their noises of elation and frustration clearly, and it calms him. His eyes are closed, and in the darkness he hears Stevonna humming, feels it through their contact.

"*Fly Me To The Moon*," Quillan mutters.

"I didn't know you know Sinatra," Stevonna says, long fingers carding through his hair.

"I didn't know you sing."

"I don't."

"Yes, you do," he smiles.

"I don't." And he can hear the amusement in her voice. "There is a distinct difference between singing and humming."

"I love Sinatra."

"So do I."

She begins to hum the song again. Another smile curls across Quillan's lips and something sparks in his mind.

"Dance with me," he says, eyes fluttering open.

Her humming stops as she looks down at him.

"What?"

"Come on," he says, getting up and pulling her to her feet,

"dance with me."

Stevonna is playing coy, tucking her face down toward her shoulder, though her smile is bright as Quillan takes her arms and arranges them, grasping her left hand in his right, their arms wrapped around each other's sides. All the while, they giggle.

"No, you have to keep humming," he says as they step around the broken patio.

"I can't," she giggles.

"No, you have to."

And she does, faltering at first, but still humming Frank's melody. They dance around the patio like children, tipping back and forth and laughing, smiles broad across their faces. Quillan can't remember the last time he felt this sort of carefree happiness. He spins Stevonna as she finishes the song and she takes his hand as they walk over to Kassia's group, swinging their arms.

"I don't get it," Kassia tells him, studying the game with frustration.

Quillan knows this game. Someone takes a set of rods and arranges them in different patterns, telling the observers that all he or she is trying to do is represent numbers. It's a tricky game, with one dead giveaway.

"Do you want a hint?" he asks.

"Yes," Kassia says petulantly. Quillan is glad she's pouty;

it means her spirit is back. He crouches down and whispers in her ear.

"Look at his hands."

He watches as Kassia pays attention, rapt with intrigue. Corey, a boy older than the rest of the group, spends a good deal of time arranging the rods in a complicated star pattern, then lays a hand flat on the ground.

"Is it five?" one of the boys asks.

"No."

"Is it three?"

"Nope."

Suddenly Kassia lights up in delight, exclaiming a series of "oh"s in quick succession.

"Is it four?" she asks.

"Yes," Corey says, picking up his hand from the ground where he had spread four fingers and rearranging the rods for another round.

"I get it!" she whispers excitedly to Quillan. "It's not the rods at all, it's how many fingers he shows on his hand!"

"I know," he says, "Five more minutes, Kassia, and then we'll go home. It's getting late. Maybe you can run the game tomorrow."

Quillan's heart sinks at the thought of home. Once again, he will leave Kassia at their aunt's with Bialas, and he will return to Lichah's futon for another night of restless sleep.

"What is it?" Stevonna asks, squeezing Quillan's hand.

"Nothing," he says, brushing off her concern.

"You should come over for dinner," she says, "I'm sure we have something."

"Really?" he says, "That would be wonderful—"

Stevonna reaches up and kisses him. It's a short kiss, not intrusive but not entirely chaste either. Quillan pulls back in surprise.

"What is it?" Stevonna says.

Quillan mouths wordlessly, a fish out of water.

"Come on, Kassia," he says, "it's time to go."

She bounces over asking for a piggyback ride, and he lets her clamber onto his back. Stevonna calls after him as he walks away, but he does not turn around. Once again, he wishes he could not listen.

"Why did Stevie kiss you?" Kassia asks as he carries her through the streets.

"I don't know," he finds himself saying, "I think she thinks things I don't think."

"Do you like her?"

"I don't know," he says again, "I like her. She's a nice person. But I don't like her that way."

"You don't *like* like her."

The juvenile phrase unwinds a bit of the tension from

Quillan.

"Do you like her?" he asks.

"Yes," Kassia says, "but I like Dana more. Are you going to get back together?"

"I don't know."

He feels stupid.

"What happened?"

He does not answer this question.

"I miss her," Kassia says, sounding awfully forlorn for a nine year-old.

"You never spent much time with her."

"I still miss her. You're sad without her."

"What about Stevonna?" he asks. "Am I sad with her?"

"Yes."

Quillan muses for a while.

"You're getting big for piggyback rides," he tells her.

"I know."

"Maybe we can go to Dana's tomorrow," he says, "Dante might have some books for you."

Quillan does not go to Lichah's house tonight. Instead, after tucking Kassia in at their aunt's, he goes to Gamma and Grand's teakettle house. He doesn't care if he has to sleep on the floor.

Cleophas is reading when he arrives. He folds the paper,

wafer-thin and limp with handling, and stores it in the pockets of his coat.

"Evening," he says softly, and Quillan has missed the sound of his voice.

"They're asleep," Cleophas answers, before Quillan can ask the whereabouts of their relatives.

"Will they mind if I stay here?"

"Of course not."

Quillan gathers up the loose chair cushions, arranging them on the floor adjacent to the sofa. He lies on his back, staring at the ceiling. He can feel Cleophas watching him from the corner of his eye.

"What happened?"

Silences seem longer in the dark.

"Stevonna kissed me."

"What did you do?"

The sound of Cleophas's voice is like the texture of some mysterious ether. It wraps around the atmosphere like a cloud, permeating every nook and cranny, like liquid silk being poured into a vial.

"Nothing," Quillan says, "I left."

"When's the last time you spoke to Dana?"

"I don't know. I told Kassia I'd take her to the Creares' house tomorrow. I don't know why."

"You want to see her again."

"But I don't know when or how. I miss that whole family," Quillan says. "I miss talking to Fontaine and reading and studying with Dante. I miss those books. I miss gardening with Alverdine in the hothouse and practicing my telekinesis. I haven't done any in ages. I want to go back to them, but I don't know how."

"Was it that bad?" Cleophas asks, "The fight?"

"Yes."

"Being in the house will help, I think," Cleophas says, "Just being in the space. Dana may not even be there."

"She may not speak to me if she is."

"Do you want her to?"

"I don't know. I don't think so."

The dark lacks insulation. Quillan feels as though Cleophas has access to his every thought.

"The scouting party leaves tomorrow," Cleophas says. "Will you be there?"

"I suppose so."

"Helminette and Redman are going."

"I didn't know."

"Do you want to move?" he asks.

"I think we have to," Cleophas replies.

"But do you want to?"

"Yes."

"Do you ever think about leaving them behind?"

Cleophas knows he means their mothers.

"I do," he says, "but I know they'd want us to go."

"It still hurts, though."

"Yeah. It still hurts."

FIFTEEN

Cleophas and Quillan watch the scouting party make their final preparations while sitting on a rock, Kassia perched beneath them. They are only some of many observers gathered before the south door to send the party on its way.

There are twenty people in the scouting party, nine women and eleven men. A boy named Leander is the youngest at twenty, while the oldest is Morena, a woman in her fifties. Their route has been mapped at this point; once out of the city, they will follow a set of abandoned train tracks up into New Hampshire. The group will ride in two hovercrafts that have lingered in the Witch Market for years. The hovercrafts are old models, but they are reliable. There is enough fuel in them for one trip only; if the move is stopped, the scouting party will have to find another way to return.

Cleophas watches as Helminette finishes loading small packets of food into one of the hovercrafts. The party has been given enough food for a week- that is all the Witch Market can afford to spare. Once the food runs out, they'll be on their own.

There are three radios between the party. None are in perfect condition, but each has a mate that will stay in the Witch Market. The radios are old, the batteries running low. The party will radio the Witch Market once every evening with a report for the day.

As the preparations come to an end, the remaining Snitches mingle with the party, saying their farewells. Cleophas hops down off of the rock and approaches Helminette. She looks older than twenty-two. Her blonde hair is braided into a single rope, and she wears a coat crowded with possessions. It's clear to Cleophas that she believes she won't be coming back to the Witch Market.

There is a grim sort of excitement all over Helminette, but it softens when she sees Cleophas. She pulls him into a hug, and Cleophas closes his eyes, breathing her in. His sister smells like lightning, sharp and cool and a bit spicy. She smells like Redman, mustard with a hint of musk, and she smells like their mother, soft and intelligent and full of life.

"I want you to have the house," she says, and Cleophas pulls back in surprise.

"With luck, we won't be coming back. You can stay there if you want. Or Quillan and Kassia can stay there— I know they're looking for a place."

"Okay," he says.

Helminette has always been taller than him. There is excitement in her eyes, and her eyes are like Brigitte's and Cleophas wonders how he never noticed that before.

"I'll see you soon," she says, giving his hands a squeeze.

"I'll see you soon," he repeats, assuring himself and hugging her again. He lets go as Gamma and Grand come over to say their farewells. Cleon, up and out of bed for the past few days despite his still-healing injury, is talking to Redman. He ends the discussion with a firm handshake. Cleophas cannot hear what he says among the moving crowd. He sees Quillan talking to Iris, and he knows Quillan is telling her about Tancred. She gives him a heartfelt embrace before moving on. It will be a great responsibility for her, being the leader, but Cleophas has faith in her. She is a strong woman, a good woman, and she will do her job well.

Cleophas watches the rest of the goodbyes wishing Blathnat could be there to hold his hand. He feels a pang as he sees Muga and Godfreya locked in a tight embrace. The wives will be split for a while, as Muga volunteered to go with the party, while Godfreya stays in the Witch Market.

When the goodbyes have ceased and the scouting party divides into the hovercrafts, the Snitches crank the south door open. It is a large process involving many people, and the south door never rises quickly. Cleophas lingers by the edge with Quillan. Part of him wants to rush out of the south door and retrieve his hoverbike from the ruins of old Boston, but he knows now is not the time. Instead he watches as the lights of the hovercrafts turn on, and they rise from the ground with a deep-throated hum. Once through the door, the hovercrafts turn left down a larger tunnel, away from the slit in the titanium sheet that hides the south door. The tunnel comes out near a freeway in Lower City. There the hovercrafts will join the flow of air traffic and ride it out of the city, breaking away later to follow the old train tracks.

But Cleophas does not get to see the lights of the hovercrafts disappear down the tunnel. The south door is closed before that. As its teeth lock into the ground, Cleophas lets out a breath he didn't realize he was holding in.

Now it's begun.

Dante is the only one home when they arrive at the Creares'. He immediately sweeps Kassia into his armchair and starts reading her *The Hobbit* and she is quickly enchanted by the story.

Quillan fetches his box out of Dana's room while Cleophas peruses Dante's extensive personal library. The man loves classic literature and mythologies as well as fantasy, and the shelves are packed with copies of everything from *Dante's Inferno* and *The Odyssey*, to carefully preserved additions of

Harry Potter and *The Lord of the Rings.*

"Darcy has my *Chronicles of Narnia,*" Dante says with irritation, taking a break from reading. "He borrowed them years ago and I've not managed to get them back yet. I'd have taken them off his hands long before now, if I had my way, but he's Alverdine's brother and she loves him, even if he is a clot."

Quillan sets his box on the table and slowly empties it, gently touching each piece. A china tea cup, cushioned by rags and painted with intricate red roses, is set beside a tin of Earl Grey. The tea wear is joined by a copy of *The Iliad,* as well as several sheets of handwriting, and a tablet. Cleophas knows the contents of the box nearly as well as Quillan. *The Iliad* was given to him by Dante for his fifteenth birthday, the sheets of paper are copies of Pablo Neruda's poems, *Ode to a Lemon* and *Ode to Salt,* and the tablet contains a copy of *The Silmarillion.* The remaining items are all toys; balls and rods and puzzles, most made of wood, but some of metal. Quillan turns one of the wooden balls over in his hand, then lets it go, leaving it bobbing up and down in midair.

Cleophas was the first one to find out that Quillan is telekinetic. They were playing a game once, when they were four and five, and Cleophas threw a wooden rod to Quillan. Instead of catching it, the rod stuck in the air right before him. Telekinesis is difficult to trace through family or culture.

There are a few more Snitches in the Witch Market with the ability, though none of them are particularly strong. The telekinesis is limited to solid, natural materials; wood, stone, dirt, plants, some metals. Fontaine, Dana's brother, is a rare exception, in which he has control only over water-based liquids.

Cleophas watches as Quillan makes the ball move around the room, roving up and down the shelves and occasionally prodding Kassia. Cleophas plucks the ball out of the air when it passes him, and he tosses it at Quillan, who stops it and sends it back. It's a game they've played for years, either with conversation or amiable silence.

The door opens and Dana enters, freezing as she surveys the scene before her. Dante stops reading about an unexpected party and gives her an inquisitive look. She does not say a word, but maneuvers the jumbled floor to her room and shuts the door.

Cleophas tosses the ball to Quillan and this time he catches it and does not throw it back.

"Helminette said you can have her house," Cleophas says, "You can use the room, since she and Redman aren't here."

Quillan nods.

"Yeah, that would be good."

He's distracted, staring at the door to Dana's bedroom. As Dante continues reading, Cleophas studies his cousin. He can see the love and longing tattooed across Quillan's face, but it seems Quillan can't. He's caught between emotions, confused and volatile. Quillan has always been drawn to Dana like a magnet; even when they argue, he runs back to her. This is something new, Cleophas realizes. Quillan is purposely restraining himself from chasing her. They hurt each other, and neither knows how to mend the wound.

"Dante, I'm going to go," Quillan says, sounding far away.

"I'll bring Kassia to your aunt's when we're done," Dante says. "Come back tomorrow though. We can pick up your Italian again."

Quillan nods. He is mute as he packs up his box.

"Quillan."

He turns to Dante.

"Take some time," Dante tells him. "You'll both come round. But you need to open yourself again."

After directing Quillan to Helminette's house, Cleophas sneaks out of the Witch Market. He takes a different route this time, slipping through a hole in the rock near the ventilation grates. Cleophas spends a lot of time beside the ventilation grates; they give off a great deal of heat and he likes to watch the steam. He's burnt his hands in it many times before, and he always forgets to change the bandages.

This particular passageway is a tight one, and it's also

uncomfortably warm. Cleophas walks sideways much of the way, his back flat against the rock. He comes out near the north door, stripping his coat off once he's free and folding it over his arm. It's been a week since he's seen Blathnat. He's always thinking about her, wondering what she's doing, what she's eating, if she's dancing, how her English lessons are going, if she's still wearing that pink coat of Salamasina's.

More than anything, he wants to give her the poem.

He knows it by heart now.

Nothing which we are to perceive in this world
equals the power of your intense fragility: whose texture
compels me with the color of its countries,
rendering death and forever with each breathing.

"*Your intense fragility,*" he repeats to himself. He likes that line a lot. It fits Blathnat well.

He is walking through the ruins of tents and huts, lying like skeletons across the ground. This is where the extermination began, up here where the scant light of Lower City filters down. It is- it was- a dangerous place to live. There are no survivors from this area. The north door is only used during emergencies, and no one inside the Witch Market knew the extermination was underway in time to open it. There are still heaps of ashes scattered among the wreckage, and Cleophas is careful to walk around them.

The incense shop in Lower City is called Rose Red. It's a favorite place of Cleophas and Blathnat. It's not clear whether or not the owner knows they are Snitches, but Maria doesn't seem to care either way.

A little bell tinkles when Cleophas opens the door to the shop, and a wall of scent descends upon him. Maria appears behind the counter, though she drops her welcoming façade when she recognizes him.

"I haven't seen you in a while," she says, the lilt in her voice different than that of the Snitches. "Where's Blathnat?"

"I was hoping you could tell me."

Maria shrugs.

"Maybe she'll be by later. Have an orange or two if you like; I over ordered," she says before disappearing into the backroom.

Cleophas takes a couple of oranges from the display and sits on a bench, observing the shop. It is a menagerie of bottles, flowers, candles, incense sticks, and fruit, all arranged in decorative mountains and towers. The mauve lighting casts a purple hue over everything; Cleophas has always felt quite enchanted here. Bouquets of flowers overflow from baskets hanging from the ceiling, their blossoms dripping down like rain. The arrangements of bottles glimmer like jewels, their liquid contents a secret. Candles, burning and unlit, are strategically placed around the shop. These ones are wax, not plastic like those the Snitches use. Cleophas wonders where Maria gets them from.

The scents though— Lord, the *smells* of this place.

Perfumes and burning incense and candles; the exotic, sugar-sweet smell of jasmine and calla lilies; the chocolate-tinged scent of orchids; sandalwood, patchouli, rose oil, eucalyptus, lavender. The smells of the spices remind him of the Witch Market- cinnamon, anise, nutmeg, ginger, frankincense. The oranges on display are studded with cloves. Cleophas plucks them out before peeling one, dropping the cloves in a sachet he keeps in his coat.

He could positively *loll* in these scents.

Cleophas sits in the shop for an hour until Blathnat arrives, opening the door with the tinkling bell and bursting in. She still has the ridiculous pink coat. She glances around wildly, not noticing Cleophas sitting on the bench, and starts examining perfumes.

"Hello," he says.

She turns around in a circle of coat and blue hair, eyes alighting on him.

"Cleophas!" she exclaims, and there is something not quite right in her tone.

Does she want to see me?

"Cleophas," she says again, trying to calm her fluttery breathing. "I, I- I didn't know you'd be here, I, I didn't—"

"Hey," he says gently, "hey. Hello."

Blathnat lets out a breath, her shoulders falling.

"Hello," she says.

"Come here," he says, patting the bench next to him. "What's going on?"

Her skin is tinted lavender under the mauve lighting, her blue hair turned violet. She is stunningly beautiful.

"Nothing," she says, "I just came from one of my lessons."

Cleophas notices that Blathnat's smell is different. Her own earthy scents are there, but her daffodil perfume is covered with heavy traces of other scents— musk and pepper and something milky. He can smell her sweat as well.

He wonders what her lessons are like.

Reaching up, Cleophas snaps a red rose from a dangling arrangement. He tucks a swath of blue hair behind Blathnat's ear, tucking the rose there as well.

"I love you," she says, and her golden eyes are honest and real.

"I have something for you," he says, pulling the poem out of his coat.

"What is it?"

"It's a poem. I want you to have it."

"I can't read that well yet, Cleophas."

"No, but I can help you," he says, "What do you know?"

Blathnat looks over the poem.

"Those are I's," she says, pointing, "And those are A's and E's and O's and — U's?"

"You've learned the vowels," he says. "Listen and let me show you."

Maria emerges to find them both poured over the paper, Cleophas's fingers underlining the words as he reads the poem aloud.

"I'm closing soon," she tells them.

Cleophas folds up the poem and presses it into Blathnat's palm.

"Keep it. It'll help you learn."

He kisses her.

They walk through Lower City together, slow-moving amongst the evening bustle. Blathnat's coat attracts a bit of attention, but otherwise they are invisible. Cleophas murmurs to her, telling her about the departure of the scouting party, how he won't see Helminette again until the move to New Hampshire. They muse about what summer will be like, away from the dirt and smog of the city. Eventually Cleophas says, "Where are you staying tonight?"

"At Salamasina's," she says.

Blathnat stays with Salamasina often. She shares an apartment with two other girls in Lower City. Cleophas doesn't know how they pay rent, but they've never been kicked out. Salamasina used to be a Snitch- still is, to a degree- but she left the Witch Market a few years ago after her parents were killed in an extermination. Snitches who leave the Witch Market are not talked about; if anything, they are looked down upon as people who abandon their culture and duty to preservation in favor of a Boxian lifestyle.

Cleophas hates to hear those discussions, especially when Blathnat is on the verge of being one of them.

"Will you help to pack, once we hear back from the party?" he asks.

"If you'd like me to," she says.

"I would."

They walk in silence until Blathnat says, "I *do* want to go, Cleophas. I don't want to stay here. I treasure my few ounces of freedom, I'd go as far as to say I like the life I have, but I want something more; I always have. The Witch Market just isn't the right place for me. I need to be out, I need to be *doing* things. I can't be constrained, and the city is the only option I have."

"I know," Cleophas says. And he does. He has always understood that about Blathnat. But knowing has never made it any easier.

SIXTEEN

On the first night, half of the Witch Market crowds into the Archive to hear the report from the scouting party.

On the second night, half of the Snitches come.

By the third night, the crowd of listeners is no longer a crowd.

Each night, Dana goes to the Archive and turns on the radio at eight o'clock. Each night, Iris radios in and gives a report on the day. They made it to New Hampshire without any error, even a little fuel to spare in one of the hovercrafts. Currently, they are ten miles from Portsmouth. Dana remembers going over the map with the party before they left.

"Manchester, Concord, and Nashua are the greatest cities," she said, pointing them out on the map, "It would be better to stay away from them, as they will have the most constant traffic with BostonMaxia. Once you're past the border, go along the coast towards Portsmouth. Many of the smaller towns have become deserted over the years; there are very few large conglomerations left in the state. Find as many resources as you can, but look at the land more than anything else.

"Once we're there, winter will arrive sooner than we think, and it will be much harsher than what we've known. We'll have the elements to contend with. If it comes to it, we may have to get help from Portsmouth and hold up there until we can build proper homes in the spring."

"Are you sure that's wise?" Morena asked.

"It has to be done," Dana said.

The Snitches' pride has always been their greatest vice. Dana knew she would have to handle it in some form.

"We have to allow ourselves to be helped," she explained, "We cannot do everything on our own. Without aid during the winter, we will just force ourselves to endure more casualties. This is why we need you to set up a base for us while we prepare to move. Find good land, old houses — strike up a relationship with Portsmouth. New Hampshire voted against the Culture Wipe; they don't have the hate for us that the Boxians do."

It worked, she thought then. She had them convinced. But now that the scouting party is gone, activity in the Witch Market has stalled. It is the waiting period, the slow road of

The Witch Market

the long game, and it seems infinitely long to Dana. She feels nailed down, the radio always a finger's width away, waiting for the call each night. Every other hour might as well be dunked in molasses, weighing her down and slowing any progress to insignificance.

At the end of the first week of waiting, Dana decides to go to the hothouse. Though it has never been a great attraction for her- Dana is a chemist and mechanic, not a gardener- she wants a distraction, scenery different than what she has locked herself into.

The hothouse is built next to the ventilation grates. Due to the lack of sunlight, heat and steam are ventilated into the hothouse to maintain its warm climate. Heat lamps hang over many of the beds, row after row of pots growing beans, peas, peppers, kale, lettuce, cucumbers, and tomatoes. In addition to the vegetables, there is a plentiful amount of herbs and flowers, as well as a few precious orange, lemon, and cherry trees.

The hothouse, like the Archive, is one of the most integral parts of the Witch Market. It is the main food source of the Snitches throughout the year, but there is only so much that can be split between so many people. Thus the Snitches resort to stealing and dumpster-diving in Lower City. The old food caches of canned meat, fruit, and vegetables, which tend to be

169

renewed every few years during a larger raid on the city, are running low. Dana suspects that she and Dante alone will drink any of the remaining wine away.

The wine is the fruit of an accident during the last scrounging, three years ago. Thinking they were busting into a meat van, the Snitches carried away twelve cases of wine, not realizing what it was until they had returned to the Witch Market. Dana started drinking when she was sixteen. She liked it from the get-go; it was not an acquired taste. Alverdine disapproved of it, but Dante had no qualms as long as she paced herself. Drinking became a pastime for the two of them; it's become a fixture in their conversations.

Stepping into the hothouse feels like sinking into a warm bath. The lights and heat lamps chase shadows into corners, and everything is lush and green. Snitches move among the beds, tending to the plants and watering. There is the sound of a broom on rough floor as someone sweeps up dead leaves and scattered dirt.

This is what we're going to have, Dana thinks. *This.*

Alverdine is sitting at the end of a bed of tomatoes. Dana walks down to her, the noise of her crutch seeming more pronounced in the clarity of the hothouse.

"Hi," her mother says as she sits down on the edge of the bed.

"Hi."

"What's going on?"

Dana had a feeling Alverdine might be here. Her mother has always been earthy.

"I needed something different," she says.

Alverdine says nothing. Her long hands are crusted with dirt.

"I feel stuck," Dana says. "I keep waiting for something big to happen, and everyone else seems to be losing interest. I wish I was out there. I wish I was exploring with them, out in the world."

She wants to say "it's no fun", but she knows that would be childish. Still, she can't help but feel petulant. She's missing out on the adventure.

"I don't know what to do. It seemed like a good idea at the time, when everyone was interested — it's still a good idea — but I feel as though I'm losing people."

"The thing about plants," Alverdine says after some consideration, "is that they can't do it alone. We have to help them grow. Much of the time it looks like they're doing nothing. It's like watching the grass grow; nothing ever seems to change when your nose is a hairsbreadth away. But we take care of them. We tend to them, water them, prune them, give them the light and heat they need to grow. And eventually, we see how much they've grown. It's a process, a long process, and you can't avoid the waiting. There's no skipping to the end. You have to stay with the plant and watch it, make sure nothing happens to it that could harm it. It needs you, even when it seems to be doing fine on its own.

"This is the waiting time, Dana, and you need to tend the Snitches. You've already planted the seed, but right now we need a direction to grow in. You have to be the one to guide us. Waiting around and doing nothing is not a solution."

"I'm not a gardener," Dana says.

"No. You're better with chemicals and machines. But the Witch Market is not so different from a machine either. Each piece has to be working for the machine to keep running. But machines need maintenance like plants need care, and we've always known you were a better mechanic."

The metaphor helps center her. She watches as Alverdine pats the soil around the tomato plants.

"Thanks, Mom."

When she gets to her feet, her mother looks up at her.

"Dana, how's Quillan?"

"I don't know," she says, and leaves.

The next few days go by much quicker. There is another meeting in the Archive, and while it is not at all as widely attended as the first, that does not matter; the necessary people are there. Most of the talk is about transport; once the scouting party radios in with a location, how will the Snitches get from point A to point B? There are three hovervans left in the Witch Market, which, once fixed up, can hold a maximum of thirty-five people. Three hovervans cannot be stretched between the remaining eight hundred and fifty Snitches. It is Grand Nicodemus who voices what everyone is thinking, that the Snitches will have to steal transport from the city. There will have to be a large party— the children and elderly omitted— who are willing to walk the tracks, as the Snitches cannot conceivably steal enough hovercrafts as it would take to transport everyone without attracting attention. The notion of the walking party is bitten, chewed up, spat out and trod upon before enough people agree that it must be done. Those walking the tracks will be given only food and camping supplies to carry. With any luck, Dana points out, the other Snitches can come back and pick them up on the way, once they have moved every person and possession safely to New Hampshire.

To Dana's irritation, talk of moving personal possessions and the contents of the Archive causes more unrest than whatever mode of transport the Snitches themselves will be taking. The Snitches' connection to their material things is cast in iron, and Dana has to work hard to lessen it. She has not yet told them that they will likely not be able to move everything from the Witch Market, as such a notion would incite a riot. Better let them come to terms with the fact in their own time, when they are confronted with the packing conundrum.

Her father, of course, figures it out right away. Dante does not speak of the problem, but Dana can see he clearly understands it in how he stands before his book shelves, somber. He reads more these days, as though worried he will never get to touch his books again. Dana doesn't know if he has decided which ones will stay when they leave the Witch Market. She knows the decision will cut him deep. Most of the books Dante owns have been passed down to him by his family; others he has collected from neglected ownership around the Witch Market. He loves each volume individually, always finding beauty and inspiration in their words.

There must be a start somewhere though, and Dana makes a point at the next meeting, that everyone must begin to look over their belongings and pick their important possessions. Most large, bulky items will have to stay- this includes furniture and some of the larger art pieces- while smaller items, like books, should be limited by weight, not quantity. For the residents who have always lived within the Witch Market, the task is a hard one. It is much easier for the Snitches who lived outside the doors before the extermination, who are used to the feeling of having to run at a moment's notice.

The other topic brought up is transportation. The Snitches cannot simply hijack one of the grocery vans while it is on its route. The authorities would raise their heads immediately. Instead they will follow the route once they have fixed their own hovercrafts, and steal them directly from the yard they retire at. There is talk about trying to build hovercrafts of their own, though that suggestion is quickly shot down due to time constraints and lack of decent materials.

The night of the most anticipated call comes quickly, now that things have been set in motion. Snitches crowd into the Archive, forming tight rings like those that surrounded the table on the eve of the meeting that started it all. Dana sits with hands clasped before her, eyes on the radio sitting in the middle of the table.

Eight o'clock comes and goes and the radio does not stir.

The silence that has built in the Archive begins to be taken down word by word, as growing whispers pass among the Snitches, high, anxious energy buzzing like a swarm of hornets. Dana sits still, watching the radio. Her face is blank.

The whispers grow louder, the swarm buzzing more and more, a tempest of sound and questions until she hears Speero yell above the mass, "Why haven't they called?"

"Maybe there was a miscommunication, maybe they think it's tomorrow night."

"There was no miscommunication, you ass, they knew what time to call."

"What if something's happened to them?"

"What if they're hurt?"

"What if the Xs got them?"

"ENOUGH," Dana roars, slamming her hand on the table.

The noise dies away like the receding tide. Dana composes herself.

"We can't tell what's happened. It may be serious. It may not be. We do not know."

Her voice is steady and low and she looks at no one in particular as she speaks.

"Tomorrow, I will be back in the Archive, and I will wait for the call."

With that, Dana takes the radio, lodges her crutch in her armpit, and makes her way through the Snitches. Behind her, she can hear the buzzing resume.

SEVENTEEN

When there is no call the next night, fear begins to take root in Dana. It starts in her stomach, like a dark rot, creeping up her body, consuming her organs, until it reaches her head and she begins to tremble. She fights it, not wanting anyone to see. She cannot appear weak. She cannot. Her mother's words resonate within her. She must be strong for the Snitches. She can almost feel Grand Nicodemus reprimanding her. She gave them all hope. What if it was for nothing?

Dana tells no one of her growing apprehensions. She would feel childish confiding in her family, even Dante, though she is sure he would try his best to help her. Cleophas is seldom around; she suspects him of sneaking in and out of the Witch Market with that girl, Blathnat.

Quillan, meanwhile, has been very present in the Creare house of late. He comes over with Kassia a few times a week, studying Italian with Dante and reading. As for Dana, he does not acknowledge her except for a few cautious glances whenever she is in the room. They have not spoken since their fight.

When Dana comes back from the Archive a third time, radio clutched in her hand, Quillan is already there, helping Alverdine make dinner. Dante wraps big arms around his wife's waist, kisses her.

"Anything?" she asks.

"Nothing," he replies.

Dana puts the radio in her room, itching to get out of Quillan's sight. She stops by Hewett, carding her fingers through the owl's feathers for a moment, eyes closed. Dante and Fontaine came along for moral support tonight, in hopes that the scouting party would radio in after two nights of silence. The number of Snitches present was few. Dana can feel their energy dwindling. Part of her wants to fade away, suddenly cease to exist, but Dana knows that is not how she functions.

"I invited Quillan and Kassia to stay for dinner," Alverdine says, as Dana reenters the room.

Dana looks to where Quillan is sautéing onions. He does nothing to allude that he is aware of her gaze.

The Creares do not have a dinner table; there is no room for one anyway, with all the clutter between the main room and the kitchen. They eat with their plates in their laps, sitting on chairs scattered around the room.

Dana stirs her baked beans around her plate absently.

Quillan sits across from her, looking down. The tension and effort taken not to engage each other is palpable. Kassia lifts her head, the movement reminiscent of Hewett, and says, "When do you think the party will radio?"

"I don't know," Dana says, "Hopefully tomorrow."

The room falls silent with the exception of the gentle murmurs that pass between Fontaine and Alverdine as they talk about the hothouse. Finally, Quillan speaks.

"What if they don't radio?"

"They will," Dana says.

"But how long are you willing to wait?"

Alverdine and Fontaine have stopped their conversation. Dana can feel everyone's eyes on her but Quillan's, who still stares at his plate. She looks directly at him and says, "I will wait as long as I have to. We're not going to stay in the Witch Market just because we missed a few calls. We're moving regardless — it's what has to happen."

"Neckarios said the move would be canceled if the party never called back," Quillan says.

"I don't care what Neckarios said," Dana replies hotly, "I'm not going to stay."

"Even if it's not safe there?"

Quillan's eyes are bright.

"It's never been safe here," Dana says. "At this rate, I'm willing to take my chances."

Despite her parents' protests, Quillan insists on helping with the dishes, so it is with great discomfort that Dana finds herself beside him, rinsing plates in the large metal basin. She can't tell what he wants from her; she knows he will speak first if there is anything on his mind, and true to her beliefs, there is.

"I know you think I think this is all a bad idea," he says, and Dana bites her tongue, "And the truth is that I can understand your reasoning, but I feel like you aren't taking everything into account."

"How so?" she says quietly.

"You're moving too fast," he says, mimicking her undertone. "There's no reason for us to be rushed to leave. I'm not saying it's a good idea to stay — like you said earlier, it's not safe here — but can't we take smaller steps?"

Frustration and fear build twin towers in Dana as she remembers what Grand Nicodemus told her about the impending extermination by the Xs. She has not told anyone his suspicions, but they resonate in her mind constantly. She will have to tell the Snitches eventually, but for now she is trying to push that time as far away as possible.

They work in silence together and are almost done when Quillan says, "I miss you, Dana."

The words hit a soft spot in her, but Dana can't help

asking, "Is Stevonna missing you?"

"I haven't slept with her," he says, dropping his voice even lower. Dana can tell she has dealt him a blow.

"Will you?"

"No!" he says. "She's too young, and even if she was old enough and we both wanted it I wouldn't, because I don't, because we both don't— I don't know what it is between us, Dana."

"Do you know what's between us?"

"I know what was," he says quietly, "I just hope it still is."

When Quillan and Kassia leave, Dana retires to her room and curls up on her bed. She always lies on her left; it best suits her bad leg. Blankets drawn up tight around her, Dana buries her head in her pillow. Her sheets don't smell of Quillan anymore; it's been more than a month since he shared her bed.

In her dreams, Dana is on top of a great cliff, rising high in the air above a dark void full of crashing sounds. Behind her are masses of Snitches; they follow her every motion as though attached to her by strings. As Dana moves closer and closer to the edge of the cliff, the Snitches twist and resent. Behind them are Xs, marching towards them in their yellow jumpsuits. Dana tries to express that the only way to safety is to walk off the cliff and fall into the void, but the Snitches balk and pull back, oblivious of the approaching Xs. With massive force of will, Dana steps over the edge of the cliff and the Snitches tumble after her, one by one.

When Dana wakes, there is another absence in her bed. The sheets around her legs are dry. She turns on a light and checks the calendar tacked to her wall, frowning. She's always on time- maybe this is just a fluke.

As the day goes by and still nothing comes, worry begins to fester in her. It's just late, she tells herself, despite the ever-present thought in her mind that she and Quillan didn't use protection the last time they had sex.

When seven thirty rolls around, Dana grabs the radio and heads over to the Archive. A few people filter in in the last half hour before eight, but the place is mostly empty. Even Neckarios is not present, but Dante and Alverdine sit next to her, studiously waiting. The minutes tick by. Eight o'clock comes and goes. Just as a few Snitches begin to peel away, at six minutes past, the radio coughs to life.

"Hello, hello— is anyone there?"

Dana lunges across the table and grabs the radio. The Snitches that have left fly back to the table and someone calls out, "Hey! THEY RADIOED!"

"Hello, yes, we're here, the Witch Market is here," Dana says, "Dana speaking."

"Dana, it's Iris. Listen, we tried to call in the past few nights, but our backups broke— they couldn't carry the distance- we had to find new batteries for our working one."

"It's all right, that's fine. Did you manage to find a location?"

"Yes, we did, it's gorgeous- Dana, it's wonderful- we're near Portsmouth still, but we've made contact with the people there and they are willing to help us settle."

"And there's room enough for all of us?"

"Yes, and there's land— it's beautiful, Dana, I wish you could all see it now."

"We will, Iris, we all will," Dana says, "We'll radio you once more, probably in about a week, and let you know when we'll leave and when we're expected to arrive."

"Okay—good luck, Dana!"

"Thank you. Thank you so much."

As the radio deadens, Dana looks up at the crowd that has swelled around her.

"We're moving the Witch Market," she says.

The response is raucous. Among the babble, Dante leans in and speaks into her ear.

"Come on," he says, "You don't have to answer these questions now. Let's go home."

For once, she lets him lead the way through the crowd.

Dana goes to sleep excited, but it is only when she is about to surrender that she remembers the other notice pressing on her agenda. I'll see tomorrow, she thinks. Then she'll figure something out.

Dana wakes herself by dry heaving over the side of her bed, her throat raw. The vomit is the only mess though, and it screams at her to reconsider.

Maybe I'm not just late.

As hastily as she can, Dana cleans up the vomit. She moves in a panic.

I need to see Cleophas. He can get me a test. Then I can be sure.

Dana stops her cleanup and slumps against the wall.

Calm down. Today is the day she needs to plan for the Witch Market. Everyone needs to get their things in order, vans need to be fixed and procured, dates need to be set. And it all has to be reasonably rushed. She can't let them know about the Xs. Not yet.

So what if she's pregnant. That's not a concerning matter right now. If there is a baby, she will take care of it. Now is time for the Snitches. She must be strong. She must lead them.

Throughout the day, Dana manages to forget her frenzy from the morning, with the exception of the small ringing reminder in her head to ask Cleophas for a pregnancy test next time she sees him. She tells no one of her speculations. No more attention should be drawn to her than necessary, and there is no need to alarm anyone.

Maybe it is just a fluke.

EIGHTEEN

Cleophas and Blathnat lay belly-down on a balcony. Far below them, BostonMaxia's Symphony Orchestra is performing in an open arena. Music is one of few things to have been exempted from the Culture Wipe; it is an eternal art, timeless and classic and modern all at once.

A woman's voice, amplified many times over, can be heard over the orchestra, performing an aria from the opera *Giulio Cesare*. The undulations in her voice remind Cleophas of bird trills, and he wonders what it would be like if birds could sing like people, and people like birds.

The owners of the balcony are out of town. Blathnat assured him that she saw them leaving, laden with luggage, before she came down to the Witch Market to fetch him. Salamasina has an actual seat, she told him. She's seeing a Boxian and he bought her a ticket as special treat.

Cleophas is content to be on the balcony. He is content to be anywhere Blathnat is.

The music is piped up through hundreds of speakers;

trembling strings, brass instruments, piano keys. Cleophas soaks in it. Music has no smell, but it electrocutes and enlivens the air, and he adores it like no other medium.

He tries not to stare too much at Blathnat. The music seems to infuse her with crystal, lighting up her skin and her hair. He feels like a magnet when near her, as though she is an idol made of iron and he cannot help but be pulled to her. He has begun to think of her pink coat as an extension of her, imagining it whenever he pictures her. He extends a finger and touches one fluffy cuff.

They recline in a beautiful un-silence, the music traveling around them, through the canals of their ears and traversing the passages of their minds and hearts like Venetian gondolas. Cleophas wishes he could braid flowers into Blathnat's hair; tulips and lilies and roses and daisies, full and bursting with color like ripe fruit.

When the aria is over and the orchestra reclaims the show, Cleophas turns to her.

"How are your lessons coming?"

He does not know much of them, only that he sees her less frequently because of them. The topic makes her visibly uncomfortable and he yearns to know why.

"They're very good," Blathnat says, each syllable a different mask. "He's going to give me projects soon, real reading practice."

He. That's news. Cleophas assumed it was a he, though Blathnat has never said anything about the gender of her tutor until now. He learned a while ago that her tutor is a Boxian as well, and that particular bit of news can't help but frighten him.

He.

"What are you going to read?"

"I wanted to start with Shakespeare, but he doesn't have any. It figures."

"Shakespeare would probably be a bit ambitious," Cleophas says, smiling. He quite likes old Will. *The Tempest* is his favorite play, along with *Midsummer's* and *Romeo and Juliet.*

"We are such stuff as dreams are made on," he murmurs.

"And our little life is rounded with a sleep. What?" she says, when he looks at her with surprise. "I'm not completely uncultured, Cleophas."

"I'm sorry," he says. Blathnat is volatile; he has to be careful not to hurt her pride. He forgets how little confidence she has in herself sometimes. She is a prideful being, with enough wants and needs to populate a hundred different lifetimes.

"Though," she says, "You do talk in your sleep. I heard it."

Cleophas blushes pomegranate red. They slept together last night, nestled into one figure on one of the broken couches in the Witch Market's junkyard. Cleophas recalls the feel of Blathnat's breath on the back of his neck, her warmth wrapped around him. They hadn't had sex. Cleophas wonders if they ever will. Part of him wants to, but the other part seems not to care. He has Blathnat and she has him. Sex is just another way to show that, and he is in no rush, not when he can show his love to Blathnat in so many other ways.

Snug in his back pocket is the pregnancy test for Dana. Thinking about it makes him feel guilty, remembering how he lifted it from a shop before they came to the balcony. He has no money, but he could not refuse Dana. If there is a baby, Quillan is the father. Cleophas knows that. It's a surreal feeling, thinking of his friends as parents, though he thinks Quillan will be a good one. Dana too, but Cleophas does not think she knows it. He hopes for her sake that she's not pregnant; she has enough to worry about.

Blathnat has rolled onto her back, her blue hair trailing over the edge of the balcony. She reminds him of a splayed lily.

"What else do I say in my sleep?" he asks, leaning closer to her.

"You recite poetry," she says, eyes like amber. "Bits and pieces of poetry. Your dreams must be like paintings."

Cleophas nestles against her, resting his head on her breasts. Every day, her words sing love in ways he never could have conceived before.

"What did I say last night?"

"Shakespeare, some. That was what I recognized. And lines of a poem, though I don't know who the author is."

"What was some of it? Maybe I can remember?"

"You talked about the preborn life and immortality and mortality."

"Akiane," he says with a smile, "Akiane Kramarik. I've shown you some of her art before. You cried when you looked at it."

"I remember now," she says, and Cleophas can hear her voice reverberate beneath him. "What's the name of the poem?

"*Returning Home*," he says, "That's its companion art piece."

Softly, he recites it with eyes closed, resting on Blathnat's chest.

"Returning Home
By Akiane Kramarik

"Inside the womb,
immortality
desires passion
of the mortality.
And the preborn life

feels the load
of the born view.

"Will audience applaud
our virtual memory
or will our memory become
our decision
apart from this life?
Who will be the ones
catching the view?

"Mortality feels so vulnerable
as it lusts
after immortality.
And it only takes
a momentary earthly tremble
to lose the memory
of the eternal perspective.

"So complex,
our broken hearts return
to their designer to be fixed.
We are all museums.
We all return to the Essence.
And today our path
is completely vertical."

Neither of them say anything as he finishes. Cleophas can hear the cogs in their brains working, can almost feel Blathnat's thought process as the poem seeps into the crevices of her mind. All around them the music swells and builds. A part of Cleophas's brain realizes that the orchestra has switched from Handel to Beethoven.

"I love you," he says.

"And I you, Cleophas."

He turns his head around and kisses her, pausing to murmur into her lips — "And I you."

Lower City is quieter than Upper City, but its noise is always greater than the Witch Market's. Cleophas and Blathnat walk down the street unabashed, blending in among the Boxians. Cleophas enjoys this feeling of anonymity- he does not experience it often. Suddenly he swells in shock, growing rigid.

"Blathnat," he says.

At the end of the street is a pair of Xs.

"Blathnat."

"I know, Cleophas."

"Let's go somewhere else."

"We'll be fine."

The Xs are walking methodically down the street.

"Blathnat."

Blathnat's coat seems like a beacon.

"Blathnat, please."

She takes his hand and pulls him behind a building, down a side alley.

"Blathnat, they'll follow us —"

She kisses him, pressing him up against the wall, fingers grappled around his collar. Cleophas dissolves under the barrage, his knees slacking. A faint thought in his head is amazed at how quickly Blathnat can unravel him, though it melts away entirely as he kisses her back.

There is nothing in the world. Only Blathnat, and the smells he associates with her. Smoke and daffodils rise from her skin, permeating with the chemical dye of her hair. Her mouth tastes of strawberry bread, sweet and bearing the promise of summer. Their mouths are like carnal hands, moving in long, languid strokes.

The Xs are long past when they finally break away. Cleophas moves a hand gently down Blathnat's cheek.

Blathnat does not go with him into the Witch Market. She says something about catching up with Salamasina, kisses him on the cheek, and runs away into the dark. The desire in Cleophas wants to reel her in, but he knows he could never accomplish that. Blathnat is too free to be controlled by any one person, and he does not want to control her.

The Creare house is quiet. Fontaine looks up from the book he's reading as Cleophas enters.

"Is Dana here?" he asks.

"In her room," Fontaine says, nodding towards the door.

Dana snatches the pregnancy test the moment Cleophas takes it from his pocket. She stares at it blankly for a minute, as though struck by the reality of the situation.

"Are you all right?" Cleophas whispers.

Dana chucks the test on her work table and begins to pace awkwardly about her room.

"Did anyone see you?"

"No, no one."

"Were there any Xs, did any Xs see you?"

"There were two," Cleophas says, surprised that she asked, "But they didn't see us. Or at least, they didn't stop us. Are you all right, Dana?"

"I'm fine. Yes, I'm fine."

She's clearly not. Cleophas waits until she paces near to him again and gently wraps his arms around her. Instantly, Dana's tension flees her body, and she slumps back against him.

"I feel as though everyone's blind, Cleophas," she says, "It's as though I'm trying to lead a group of blind, deaf, and dumb people. I can't begin to go the same way. I feel like I'm losing control."

Cleophas tightens his arms around her, resting his chin on her shoulder. He is the only one Dana would ever admit this to.

"I believe in you," he says.

"I know you do." And he can hear the wincing smile in her tone. "But I need more than just you."

"It'll work out, Dana. You need to trust in yourself more. It'll all be fine. We'll all make it to New Hampshire and we'll —" he bites his lip, looking for the right word.

"It's not that we're starting over. We're going to continue."

Dana traces a heart on his hand.

"Thank you, Cleophas."

When they were little, Cleophas and Dana would constantly trace hearts on each other. It is their private way of showing their care for each other. Dana hasn't given Cleophas a heart in years. He hugs her tighter and presses a kiss into her hair.

On the route back to the Ektoses' house, Cleophas can't help but think of the time Quillan is spending with Neckarios's daughter, Stevonna. He knows Quillan would never be intentionally unfaithful to Dana, but he also knows how easily he can be swayed. Quillan has always been an easy one to tempt. Stevonna is a sweet girl, but she is not right for Quillan. Still, he sees the two of them together often, Stevonna hanging onto his arm or playing with Kassia, who now seems to be as attached to Quillan as an extra limb.

He wonders what the result of the test will be, and if Dana will tell Quillan if they are positive. Cleophas already knows though, that if they are, Dana will tell no one. That is how she is, how she always has been.

Her worry bothers him though. He has always known Dana to be a confident person, and her lack of self-assurance is curious. Of course, Dana has never undertaken so massive a task as trying to move the Witch Market, but she has the capability to do so. Still, Cleophas has an inkling that her worry is not rooted entirely in the move, or in the possibility of a pregnancy.

All of the sudden, the memory of his and Blathnat's near encounter with the Xs materializes. He's not used to seeing the Xs in Lower City. In fact, he hardly ever sees them or their pods anywhere but during an extermination or patrol of old Boston. It's strange that Dana asked him. As much as she berates him about his trips into the city, she rarely asks about the Xs.

What does that mean?

Cleophas stops dead, hovering beneath a green lantern.

Why would Dana ask about the Xs? Why is she so worried?

What does she know about the Xs?

NINETEEN

Dana waits three days before using the test. When she does, and the little red plus sign gleams at her like a brand mark, she disposes of the test herself and tells no one.

I'm pregnant, she thinks. *Shit, I'm pregnant.*

Once the shock dies away, Dana tries to bury her concern. Of course, the truth will come out when she can no longer hide it, but that will not be for months. This is not her primary concern; there are other, more important matters on her plate.

There have been whispers of more sightings of Xs, mostly from people brave enough to leave the Witch Market for food. Not enough for anyone to make anything of it, but enough to comment on. Grand Nicodemus knows what it means though, and now Dana does too.

Something needs to be done.

Amid all of the preparation for the move, the packing and filing and minimizing, defenses need to be set up. In case the Xs come early, before the move is complete, the Snitches need to have some way to protect themselves.

Dana can't do this alone.

"Dad?"

Dante looks up from a file he is scrutinizing. He looks tired.

"What is it?" he asks.

"I need your help."

"What with?"

Dana moves a pile of papers off of a chair and sits down, angling her leg carefully.

"Do you remember on the night of the very first meeting, when Grand Nicodemus stayed and talked to me afterwards?"

"Yes," Dante nods.

"He talked to me about the Xs. You've heard what people have been saying, about the sightings?"

"I have, yes. What did Grand Nic tell you?"

"He said that he's seen a lot. He said that he's seen increased activity of the Xs for years now. He thinks they'll break into the Witch Market before the end of the summer."

Dante sits back in his armchair. After a moment he runs a hand through his dark hair. There are faint streaks of silver in it, running back from his ears like veins of ore in a mine.

"What do you think?" Dana asks.

"I think I agree," Dante says, "I don't want to agree. I'd rather not acknowledge it at all, but I agree. Jesus, it's a frightening thought."

He runs his hand through his hair again.

"And I suppose you have something in mind, something to do about it?"

"I do," Dana says, "But I need help."

Dante nods.

"Hang it," he says, getting up, "First we need wine."

Dana waits patiently as he snatches up a couple of empty glasses from around the room and disappears into the kitchen, returning again with full glasses and the bottle to boot.

"So," he says, handing Dana a glass, "The Xs are going to break in by the end of the summer. What do you have in mind?"

"Well, we need to set up some sort of defense, but it can't be wide spread," Dana says, "Or at least it can't be obvious to everyone. We can let a select group know, but that's it."

"You don't want to incite a panic."

"Exactly."

"Do you have any ideas already? There are a lot of different tactics you could use."

"There are some more basic ones I thought of," Dana says, "Involving the current prep. People are going out to the tent planes more and more often, and we can't risk the Xs coming by for an impromptu extermination. We can enforce that people go in groups, and for short periods of time, an hour max. We also need to make sure those going to get food and vans are properly armed, in case anything becomes nasty."

"And what about for the Witch Market itself?"

Dana takes a drink and stares into the depths of her glass.

"I want to build a barricade. I want to gather parts from the junkyard and old Boston, and build a barricade in front of the south door. And I want to start making explosives again."

"You know that's not a good idea, Dana," Dante says, putting his glass aside.

"I don't know," she counters, "I know what's right and I know what's necessary. We need weapons."

"Last time you played with explosives—"

"I don't *play* with explosives, Dad, and I don't need to be reminded of what happened. I haven't made anything major since my accident, but I've still been working. We need to be able to defend ourselves."

"Dana, you aren't as careful as you think you are," Dante protests.

"But I can't always be careful," she replies, "I have to take chances, otherwise nothing would ever get done. Joan would agree with me."

"Joan of Arc was not an amateur chemist," Dante retorts.

"No. But she was a year older than I am when she was burnt at the stake," Dana says, "She knew what she had to do and she did it, regardless of the cost."

It is not often that Dana and her father butt heads. They get along too well, despite their differences. Dante has always loved history more than her, but Joan of Arc is Dana's favorite historical figure, and she brings her in as a support whenever they argue.

"Joan of Arc followed her faith in God," Dante says. "You don't have that."

"Nor was I born in France in the fourteenth century," Dana says. "But we both share drive. We do what must be done, and we have to trust ourselves to do so. I have faith in myself. I know what I have to do."

"Fine," Dante says, slumping in his armchair, defeated, "So you'll make bombs and grenades and such; anything else?"

"I'm going to finish working on my electric stick," she says, "I'm nearly done; then I think we can replicate some more of them."

"And what about this barricade, why only before the south door?"

"The Xs know about the south door now, but they don't know about the north door," Dana explains, "We need the north door free in case we have to flee in an emergency."

"Fair enough," Dante amends, "Now to the gritty matter: who do you want to tell?"

"I'd like to leave Neckarios out of it," she says.

"I as well, but we both know he'll find out about it eventually," Dante says, taking a drink. "So do you leave him in the dark and weather his outburst when he finds out what's been going on under his nose, or do you tell him and use his aid, even if he is an irksome bug?"

"I suppose we'd better tell him," Dana says begrudgingly.

"Best let Aunt Alanza know," Dante suggests, "She'd be good for this. And tell Quillan's Aunt Karin, too."

"You don't like her."

"Yes, I know, but Karin doesn't get along with most people. However, she'd still be an asset."

"I'd like to involve some of the people who wanted to be in the scouting party. There were a lot of good people, and we could use their hands."

"Yes, that's a good idea. How would you like to let them know?"

"I'll have to do it privately, I suppose," Dana says, "I don't want anyone to know who shouldn't. The less rumors flying around, the better. We can't meet at the Archive like we normally do; that would be too obvious."

"Speaking of the Archive—I don't mean to change the subject, but this is important— have you considered how all its contents is to be packed away?"

"No," Dana says, "I'd forgotten I had to do that."

"There's a lot you have to do, Dana," Dante says with a wry smile, swishing his wine around its glass. "I can understand that some of it must slip your mind at times. Just let that one stew for a while. It's a biggie."

"How are we supposed to move the entire Archive?" Dana exclaims, letting loose for once.

"I don't know, you tell me."

"I'm just a teenager."

"And Joan of Arc was a teenager when she became a revolutionary and was burnt at the stake," Dante says, "You can't back away from this now, Dana. It's a huge job you've put on your shoulders. Your mother and I, we can help you with directions, but you have to be the driver, and often times that means you have to improvise. But you don't have to do it alone."

"So do I call a meeting?"

"I don't know, do you want to?"

"Not particularly, no."

"Do you want to know what I'd do?"

"You'd call another meeting."

"I'd call another meeting."

"We can't bring everything, though, we just can't. Prints and papers and scans, yes, but bulky items— there's no way we can transport all of it, unless people are willing to try and steal more vans. Even there I have to put my foot down; it's too dangerous to steal large amounts of transport."

"You may be surprised what the Snitches will be willing to do to preserve what we have," Dante says.

"Dad," Dana says, speaking as gently as she dare, "We can't bring it all."

Dante is quiet for a long moment, intently examining his glass.

"I know," he says eventually, quiet and somber. "Believe me, Dana. I know."

It is one evening when Dana is finishing her rounds, having called on those chosen to inform them of the Xs and defenses for the Witch Market, that she sees them. She ducks behind a house as quickly as her leg allows, peering out from the safety of the shadows to watch. Her heart has leapt into her mouth without warning, and she can feel it balanced precariously on her tongue.

Quillan and Stevonna are walking down the gravel street, stepping in and out of the lantern light. She is holding onto his arm, laughing at something he's said. She's a pretty girl, decked out in some blue lace that must have belonged to her mother or grandmother. Quillan looks happy.

He never looks that happy with me —

Stop it, Dana tells herself. She's had beautiful times with Quillan. Wonderful times. Her memory flicks back to the shiny red plus sign, and she winces sadly. Wonderful times.

I want him back.

Visions blossom in Dana's head of her approaching Quillan and Stevonna, ripping the girl's hands from him and slapping her silly. She shakes her head. Is this jealousy? It feels so rich and potent and angry, but also wounded, like a great animal that has been hurt many times over.

I want him back, she thinks, and the admittance stings like alcohol on a cut. She feels as though she is dissolving, weakening like a plant without water, and she watches the pair of them walk by. He's walking her home. She wonders if she will kiss him goodnight, or if he will kiss her. The thought makes her stomach twist, and Dana chokes on her own breath for a moment as heat and the prequel of tears knot in her throat. For the first time in her life, Dana feels utterly alone.

Quillan

TWENTY

The date for the move is July thirty-first. The Witch Market has been set in motion. People are rarely still nowadays; there is a bustle to the Witch Market that Quillan has never seen before, much less been a part of. Every few days parties embark for the ruined tent planes to scavenge what items they can find among the wreckage. Stolen grocery vans are being flown in each week; there are six of them now and there will be nine when the three broken ones inside the Witch Market are fixed. The Archive and the hothouse are like hives, constantly buzzing with people as the Snitches try to figure out how to pack away all their worldly treasures and necessities.

Quillan has been designated as part of the walking party. He wanted Kassia to ride in the vans with their disengaged father, but she refused to be parted from him. After a tussle, he relented and agreed that she could walk with him. Neckarios wanted to protest, but Quillan informed him in no small terms that Kassia will be walking with him and that is that.

Neckarios has been taking the reins far more than usual lately. He can be found everywhere, organizing and ordering and doing what he believes to be best. Quillan is not particularly fond of the man, but he knows he means well.

Neckarios's increased activity also goes to highlight how much less Dana is seen. Whenever Quillan is at the Creares', she is always shut in her room. He knows she's working- it's easy to deduce from the smells and noises that emanate from her door- but he doesn't know why.

Stevonna is still spending ample time with him. His rebuke of her kiss in the junkyard has done little to lessen her obvious affections toward him. She has taken to coming around Aunt Yeva's house when he is there, and Bialas has actually grown quite fond of her, which causes mixed emotions for Quillan. Part of him wants to care for his father himself, while the other is grateful for the life she brings out of Bialas. He has started speaking again, and the few times he makes conversation with Quillan, he makes a point to touch on "that sweet young thing". Quillan can't help but agree with him on that. Stevonna is a charming girl. Sometimes he catches himself looking at her for long stretches of time, and he chastises himself for his easy heart.

He's not in love with her though. He's not.

He still freezes when she kisses him— and she has kissed

him multiple times now — and the most romantic thing he does on his part is hold her hand on occasion.

Stevonna does things to him that no one else has done before. She intrigues and mesmerizes him. He appreciates her and is confused by her, is attracted to her and at the same time wants to stay as far from her as possible.

He has taken to walking her home in the evenings after tucking Kassia in at Helminette's old house. The new rhythm of the Witch Market lessens at night, though people are still trickling in and out of the Archive as they pass it. Stevonna grasps his hand, swinging it slightly between them. Quillan catches himself staring again, watching the lantern light reflect in her yellow hair, and blinks his eyes rapidly, jerking his head away and looking straight ahead.

Speero passes them in the street and gives Quillan a particularly dark look.

"What was that about?" Quillan murmurs, after he's passed.

"Speero?" Stevonna says, "He's had a crush on me for ages. Don't worry about it."

Quillan blanks. Competition for Stevonna's affections is nothing he wants any part of.

Neckarios's house is the largest in the Witch Market, built from the ruins of an old restaurant. Its architecture is angular and copper. Lamps curl from its many surfaces like distorted lily of the valley blooms, and the double front door is big and wide. It's a large house for only two people. Stevonna's mother died in an extermination years ago.

Quillan and Stevonna stop outside the door. Per Quillan's unspoken request, they do not go inside. So far, he has declined every opportunity.

"Thanks for walking me home," Stevonna says, looking up at him sweetly. She stretches up on her tiptoes and presses her lips against his. The kiss is a short one. Once again, Quillan does not respond to it. He relaxes the moment she slumps down, and squeezes her hand gently.

"Good night, Stevonna."

"Night, Quillan. I'll see you tomorrow."

He waits until she has closed the door before leaving.

Quillan finds himself walking to the south door unconsciously as he leaves, Stevonna and the kiss still on his mind. Never has he felt the urge to kiss her back, but now as he walks away, he can't help but feel the tiniest impulse arising, and he wonders what it would be like.

No.

His subconscious rears and bats him around the head.

No, he thinks. He couldn't. He wouldn't. He has Dana, or he did.

That thought alone is enough to distress him.

He's going to the tent planes, it's decided. He doesn't care that he's unarmed, or that he's not going with a group during one of the designated times. He could not care less about the new regulations. Right now he wants a piece of home, and no matter how much time he spends inside it, the Witch Market itself will never be that.

Luckily, the south door is still open. It will be cranked shut soon, but he can always use the Arandas' chute to get back inside.

The area is reminiscent of a wasteland as Quillan emerges from the slit in the titanium sheet that conceals the south door. The scant artificial light that seeps through from Lower City lights up the abutments of transparent alumina that spit the landscape, giving Quillan just enough light to survey the plane.

Immediately before him, fallen and sloped like sand dunes, are the chain link fences and stretches of plastic mesh. Quillan's pinky finger itches as he steps over the mesh, remembering how Tancred broke his hand and then cut off the tip of his finger with a pocket knife, only to fall dead the moment after. There are still piles of black ash scattered about. They grow more and more frequent as Quillan makes his way towards the overpass, and the shapes of crumpled tents and scrap houses loom like strange hunchbacked figures. The silence is incredible.

Quillan doesn't like looking at the ashes. Twice, he accidentally steps in a pile only to leap away, cursing and choking back a sudden whirlwind of emotions and dust. He tries his hardest not to think of the ashes of his mother and sister, bottled back at Aunt Yeva's house.

It takes him a while to locate what is left of the Oddanies' tent. As he walks amongst the ruins, Quillan remembers how the scene used to look. The southern tent plane was a bright place; at least, as bright as any place could be, down in the dark under the city. It was strung with lanterns like those that hang in the Witch Market, paper pots that shed amber across the homes of the Snitches there. The tents and houses were small and shabby, but well-kept and tidy. Everyone knew everyone else's business, and Quillan remembers waking up to the sound of children running between the intricate pathways over the pavements.

Now the area about the overpass is dark and mutilated, ravaged by the Xs. The Oddanies' tent, which used to stand tall and vibrant, now lies on the ground like a trampled balloon. Quillan feels his muscles stiffen as he walks around it. He lifts the canvas tenderly, as though it is a living skin, peering beneath it. The family cots lie broken on the ground. There are three; one for his parents, one for the Ks, and one for himself. Their folding tables and chairs are as equally damaged, but Quillan picks up one of the chair cushions and hugs it to his chest. Grainne used to embroider often; it was her most favorite hobby. Her needle touched most of the fabrics they owned. She used to label the Ks' clothes so they wouldn't mix them up, and as Quillan grew older, she sewed Q's onto his collars and cuffs, as Bialas had a habit of grabbing his shirts instead. This seat cushion slip cover has a bear cub embroidered on it, a Rubix cube between its paws. She sewed it for Quillan for his eleventh birthday, for his name which means "cub" in Gaelic, and for his love of puzzles.

After a second thought, Quillan gathers up the other seat cushions and strips the slips from them. Kassia and Klaudia's are both embroidered with daffodils embossed with a K, though Kassia's daffodil is pink. Quillan will have as much of his family as possible. He caresses Grainne and Klaudia's slip covers before piling them with the others.

Klaudia's blanket is charred; it falls to pieces when he touches it. Carefully, he picks up the one corner that remains intact, folds it, and pockets the fabric. Poor Klaudia, who was born with a crippled leg, who was so fierce and vibrant and alive. No more.

He has found Kassia's stuffed animal fish and is looking through his father's collection of crosswords when he hears a rustle.

Catherine Geiger

"Who's there?" he calls out, then feels foolish. Though his eyes have adjusted to the dimness, it is still incredibly dark. He wonders for a moment if it is just a rat, but no. Rats sound different.

Now Quillan regrets not bringing a weapon.

Quickly, he picks up the longest of the snapped tent poles, hefting it like a lance before him.

"Come out!" he says, "I know you're out there."

After a moment, the noise returns, and a shape begins to move from behind a heap. There is a different noise, a crackling noise, followed by sharp bluish-silver light. Quillan raises the pole, his heart pounding.

"Don't, Quillan!"

Quillan almost drops the pole.

"Dana?"

She hobbles into view, crutch under one arm, a long metal stick in the other.

"What are you doing out here?" he asks.

"What are you doing out here?" she hisses, seething.

"You followed me," he realizes, "Why the hell— Dana—"

"It's not safe, Quillan," she says.

"I know that, Dana, thanks," Quillan says, "But I needed to go."

"So what, if an X came along you could defend yourself with a fucking tent pole?"

216

"That's not the point—when did you finish that?" Quillan asks, pointing at the metal stick in her hand.

"A few days ago," Dana says, knocking her electric stick against a pile of rubbish. It crackles with light menacingly. "This is just the prototype; we're going to make more of them."

"We?" Quillan says, "Who's we?"

"Just some people."

"Just some people? Dana, do you think you have some secret organization going on right now? Because it's a lot more obvious than you think. You spend all this time in your room working on God knows what—of course I think you're up to something. That and these new rules about leaving the Witch Market—and don't think I haven't noticed what's going on in the junkyard. You're not just pulling parts for the vans. I haven't figured that out yet, but whatever it all is, you might as well just tell me, because I'm going to find out eventually and I'm worried—" Quillan stops, cutting himself off before he lets out more than he intends to.

Dana is quiet. Even in the dark she avoids his eyes.

"You really want to know," she says, and her tone catches him.

"Dana," he says, "How bad is it?"

"The Xs are going to try to break into the Witch Market," she says, "Not just try, they'll succeed."

Quillan takes a moment to register this.

"How do you know?" he asks.

"Grand Nicodemus told me," she says, "He's seen it, watched it all happen over the years. And even now- you've heard what people have been saying. The sightings are more frequent. And they know about the south door now. So that's what we're trying to do, a small group of us. We're readying defenses against the Xs. We're going to build a barricade from pieces in the junkyard. Hopefully it'll be something."

"Who knows?" Quillan asks, "Who knows, so far?"

"My dad," Dana says, "Neckarios. A few of our relatives; my Aunt Alanza, your Aunt Karin. Frode, Gina, Murrow, Rutland. Mostly people who wanted to go on the scouting party."

"Jesus," Quillan mutters. He takes a few steps in a random direction and back, trying to center himself. "Why'd you follow me?"

"Why do you think, Quillan?" Dana says.

The atmosphere between the two of them is something verging on tender. It's a palpable thing they are both scared to touch. Dana's electric stick crackles again, the same bluish-silver light splitting from it.

"Can you make it stop doing that?" Quillan asks, "Someone might see it."

"Let's just go back, Quillan," Dana says, "It's not safe out here, that's why I came after you."

"Fine," Quillan acquiesces. He gathers up the slip covers and Kassia's toy fish.

"Come on," she says, "We have to get back before they close the south door. I can't use the Arandas' chute."

They walk as quickly as Dana's lame leg will allow. There is an elephant between them that burgeons with each step, as the words they do not say weave an intricate tapestry. They were never like this before, never this bad. They didn't need to speak to each other to communicate. Communication is what broke them apart, but it may be the only thing that will mend them.

I miss her, Quillan thinks. *I miss her.*

His want to tell her is so big it hurts, but it does not feel right. Still, he wants so desperately to be honest, to stop hiding.

I love her.

"Dana," he says.

He reaches for her arm, but only brushes her sleeve before she recoils. He expects to see anger in her eyes, but there is only a remarkable sadness.

"What are we doing, Quillan?" she says.

Quillan swallows. *Here we go.*

"I love you, Dana," he says.

"I know. I love you too," she says, and he has never heard

her sound more sad. "But what are we doing? What is this?"

"I don't know," he says, sounding desperate.

"Can we have this conversation another time?" she asks, walking again, "We have to get inside."

"No, we can have it right now," he says, walking up beside her. "I love you, Dana. You know it, I know it; we love each other. Why can't we be together?"

"Why do you think?" she explodes, all barriers gone. "It's because of that stupid girl, it's because she hangs on you day and night, and you're too thick to see that she's infatuated with you because she thinks she's found a new toy, because you're her shining knight, and because you're so easy to sway and tempt and one day you might kiss her back, because I know, I know she kisses you!"

"I don't love her, Dana," Quillan appeals, "I don't care about her that way."

"But you do care about her!"

"Yes, I do, I care about a lot of people, it's how I am! She's sweet and kind and I like her, but I don't *love* her, Dana, I love *you*."

"But she kisses you."

"Yes, I'm very aware of that, thanks—do you think I like it? I don't know what to do when she kisses me, as you seem to very well know."

"But you're so easy, Quillan," Dana protests, "You've

always been easy. You're so easily devoted and you're such a romantic, and I can't help imagining that one day she'll pull you and tease you and you will kiss her back. And you don't know either, that's why you're so uncertain. You don't know if you will or you won't, and don't try to deny it, because I know you. I know you damn well, and we can't do this, we can't be together while you're still uncertain. It hurts me, Quillan, it fucking hurts."

"I never meant to hurt you," he says, shocked.

"I know you never meant to," she screams, and he realizes there are tears streaming down her face. "Quillan, I want you. I want you back. I've come out of my shell, I'm back out in the open, but I need you to fix this, because this is one thing that I can't fucking fix as hard as I try and as much as I want to and there's so much that I have to do and I want you back in my life, but I can't have you while you're with her."

"Dana, I—"

She whirls around and slaps him across the face.

"I'm sorry," she yells, still crying, and he tries to wrap her in his arms but she fights him and twists away, picking up her crutch and disappearing through the slit in the titanium sheet. He can hear the south door being cranked shut as he follows her, and only just makes it in time, her words and sobs ringing like crystal bells in his head.

TWENTY-ONE

In the morning, Quillan wakes Kassia by surprising her with her toy fish. It's an old, soft thing, a baby toy, but Kassia is elated by it and hugs him tightly. When Quillan takes her to Yeva's house for breakfast, the fish sticks out of her dress pocket. Their father is sitting at the table eating canned peaches when they arrive.

"New delivery," Aunt Yeva explains as Kassia squeals over the fruit, "It was just brought in yesterday."

They are sitting down when Bialas looks up slowly, his movements like some sedated animal. His eyes cast around, looking for someone who is not there. Then he turns to Quillan and says, "Where's that girl? The sweet young one. She's not here."

"No, Dad," Quillan says, "Stevonna's probably at home."

"Oh," Bialas says, "You should bring her around more often. I like her."

"I don't know if I'll be bringing her much anymore, Dad," Quillan says, and the words are strained in his throat.

"Why?"

For a moment, Bialas sounds like a child and Quillan winces.

"I don't know," he says, "I think Dana might be coming more often."

"Oh. All right."

As they resume eating, Bialas's eyes travel around the room again. Quillan is watching out of the corner of his eye when Bialas's gaze alights on Kassia. He smiles slowly, big and sunny.

"Hello, Grainne," he says.

Instantly, the mood changes. Kassia begins to whimper and reaches for Quillan, who ditches his chair and picks her up where she begins to sob into his shoulder. Surprise and confusion are written across Bialas's face, and as he begins to open his mouth to speak, Yeva takes a firm hold of his wrist and says, "It's okay. Quillan and Kassia are just going out for a little walk. Finish your breakfast."

Quillan carries Kassia outside and they sit down against the wall of the house. Kassia quiets some, but still clings to him, cuddled against his chest. For the first time since the extermination, Quillan is angry at his father. All irrational thoughts of his ailment spill forth. How can he do that to Kassia? How dare he call her their mother's name? Kassia has already pushed the memory of the extermination behind her-she needs no further reminder of the losses she has endured. And Bialas — why can't he get ahold of himself?

I need a father, too.

How long will he stay like this? How long will he be this shell, this ghost of a man? And now that Quillan's told him Stevonna won't be coming back- which maybe she won't, after today- how far will that set him back? Will he retract?

Quillan berates himself for his thoughts. He can't expect this from his father. Bialas will come round in his own time, or never. He should be grateful for what improvements he has made already. At least now he is far less comatose and his nightmares have lessened significantly. Quillan sighs.

"I need to do something today, Kassia," he says.

"What?" she asks, head poking up like a turtle.

"I can't tell you that," he says, shaking his head, "And you can't come with me. Where do you want to stay today?"

"Not here."

"We do have to go back inside though."

"Why?"

"Because it's not Dad's fault he's like this. He's sick. You know that, right?"

Kassia nods.

"Just give him a hug, Kassia. He loves us very much, Mummy too. He just forgets sometimes that she's not here."

"And Klaudia?"

"And Klaudia."

"Quillan, can I go to Dana's house today? Dante's still reading *The Hobbit*."

"Sure. Come on, up you get," he says, pulling her to her feet.

Aunt Yeva is still consoling Bialas when they walk inside.

"I don't understand," he says, wounded and confused, "What did I do?"

"Nothing, it's all right," Yeva says, rubbing his arm.

Quillan gives Kassia a gentle poke in the back; she walks over to Bialas and hugs him. It's an awkward embrace at first—Kassia is tense and Bialas still confused—but soon both parties warm to it and Kassia settles on her father's lap and whispers an "I love you" in his ear.

Quillan coughs.

"I have to go," he says. "Thanks for breakfast, Aunt Yeva."

"Any time," she says, "Is Kassia going with you?"

"Not with me, but she's going to the Creares today. We'll see you tomorrow probably."

"Are we leaving now?" Kassia asks, jumping down.

"Yes. Come on, let's go."

"Don't worry," Yeva tells him in an undertone, "I'll look after him."

Quillan does not go inside when he drops Kassia at the Creares'. He declines Alverdine's invitation and her offer of a drink, and proceeds on a course to Neckarios's house. He does not know if Stevonna will be there, or if she will be in the Archive, but this route takes him by both places. Ultimately, it is she who finds him first, wandering outside the Archive.

"Quillan!" she says, running up to greet him. She is especially pretty today and Quillan's stomach knots itself.

"Hi," he says. Gingerly, he touches her shoulder. "I need to talk to you."

They lead each other behind the Archive, Stevonna's fingers tangling with his. Quillan feels like the earth, as though Stevonna is the moon orbiting him. She looks up at him with big blue eyes, crystal and so, so bright. Quillan's stomach is a pretzel.

"I—" he says, but he falters, stopping himself.

How do I do this?

He can see her watching as he fights for proper words, and a soothing expression washes over her face.

"Hey," she says. "It's okay."

Her hands are on either side of his face now, and in a moment she is kissing him. Finally, Quillan acquiesces. He returns the kiss with vigor, soaking Stevonna in like sunlight. His hands grab her shoulders and he can hear her breathing, the rush of blood through her veins, her heartbeat fluttering like a bird. She tastes like sugar and peaches and Quillan kisses her almost wildly. Stevonna is more than a willing participant, and it is Quillan who is the first to break away. They have backed up against the Archive, Quillan's hands still resting on Stevonna's shoulders, their foreheads brushing together as they catch their breath.

"Are you okay?" Stevonna asks, "You're trembling."

Quillan takes a deep breath.

"I can't do this, Stevonna," he says, and every muscle in his body seems to clench. "It's not right."

"What do you mean?"

He can hear the incredulity threatening in her voice.

"I mean it's not right. I should have stopped a long time ago. I never should have let you get close enough to kiss me."

"Is there someone else?"

There it is. The incredulity. She's broken away from him now, and he can feel her stare burning him.

"We were never together, Stevonna. I don't know what we had, but we were never together, not really. At least not that I felt. I'm sorry if I led you on, I truly am-"

"Shut up," she says. "Just shut up."

She shudders. He steals a glance at her and sees that she's crossed her arms defiantly.

"What, did you think you could just *use* me?"

"I never used you," he exclaims. "You kissed *me*, Stevonna, not the other way around!"

"That's not how it was just then!"

"If you were in my position, what would you have done?"

"I would have told the truth!"

"Stevonna, what truth could I tell you?" Quillan asks, "You knew a story I didn't. Whatever you thought about us, I wasn't in on. It was my mistake not to clarify it all in the beginning, but I liked you—I do like you. You've helped my family and you've helped me—"

"But what you're saying is that you were never in love with me?" she interrupts.

"I care about you, Stevonna. I do," Quillan says gently, "But I've been in love with someone else since I was ten years old and I don't think that will ever change."

"Fuck you," Stevonna says, and he sees that tears are gathering in her eyes. There is that terrible catch in her voice of those people about to cry. He knows now an "I'm sorry" will do nothing. He has done what he meant to do, and while it has hurt, there is nothing more to it.

Dana is in her room building a gas bomb when Quillan returns to the Creares'.

"Hi," he says.

"Hey."

She doesn't ask him what happened. He knows she expects him to tell her on his own, so he does.

"I was just with Stevonna," he says. "She kissed me. And you were right, I did kiss her back, but it made me realize what she thought was between us, and what really wasn't. I love you, Dana. You know I do. I love you more than I can possibly express. And I have always been yours, but I didn't realize how I was others' too. I've fixed that now."

He stops, words trickling away from him. Kneeling before her, Quillan takes a hold of her hands in her lap, treating them like birds with broken wings.

"I forgive you," Dana says, watching their hands.

Quillan's eyes know no bounds as he looks at her; she is the most beautiful creature. He has always known Dana to be real. He could never desire an angel, not when Dana is so incredibly, beautifully human. She kisses him over their hands, and Quillan opens like great drapes pulled from a window in winter. It is their first kiss in over a month, and Quillan feels whole again. The kiss is soft, nearly chaste, like roses opening.

"You kiss by the book," Dana whispers.

Quillan smiles against her mouth.

"But Juliet, isn't that where all the best come from?"

TWENTY-TWO

The parade winds through Upper Boston, coursing down the invisible streets of air traffic like a great shimmering caterpillar. Banners bigger than bed sheets trail behind the moving floats and platforms, billowing like lungs. It is a balmy night, and the breeze is warm with the promise of summer. Cleophas and Blathnat sit on a ledge next to the recently retrieved hoverbike, fingers like bits of lace sewn together. With every gust of air, Blathnat's hair blows about her head in a curtain of blue.

Across the country, the annual New Culture Celebration is occurring. The New Culture Celebration is Cleophas's favorite time to be in the city. Despite the tragedy it has caused him, he does not heavily resent the Culture Wipe; he understands why it was done. The New Culture Celebration is recognition of the contributions made over the past year to the culture of BostonMaxia and the United States as a whole.

The parade is a bazaar for the senses. The floats pass by in segments, each devoted to a different genre of culture. Science is first, followed by fashion, film, dance, art, food, scents, and literature. Music resounds over all, weaving among the lights and cheers and yards of fabric and glitter that preside about the floats like a cloud.

Cleophas has been waiting for hours to see the latter part of the parade, for the food and scent featured floats are an olfactory heaven. They pass by like giants, the food floats tiered like wedding cakes or molded like cornucopias, issuing different colored steams or shining with thick glazes. Cleophas sees one cake the size of a taxi, covered with thousands of tiny electric lights buried in frosted roses. Towers of waxed fruit and fondant stand in intricate formations, mimicking the monuments of BostonMaxia. Cleophas spots one that looks like the Cassiopeia.

As the scent-themed floats begin to approach, Cleophas tries to be excited, but there is something else on his mind. Blathnat is being unusually quiet this evening, her laughter forced and faint; she is not herself. Cleophas looks at their hands, like spiders trapped in each other's webs, and he feels strange.

"Blathnat," he says quietly, "What's wrong?"

He can see her profile, so close to his own, as she looks down on the parade. The smell of lilies begins to enter his nostrils, sweet and soft, emanating from the floats. He can see a glimmer in Blathant's golden eyes, the sheen of tears about to fall.

"Blathnat?" he whispers. He is afraid to speak, as though he will break her with a single syllable.

She turns to him, and the tears brimming in her eyes threaten his heart. He chokes.

"I need to tell you something," she says, "Something that's been on my mind for a long time now."

Her hand feels cold in his, and he rubs his thumb against it.

"My English tutor's name is Roi," she says, "When Salamasina told me about him, I didn't have any money. I still don't. I had no way to pay him. So we came up with a compromise between the two of us. He would teach me to read and write, and in return, I would do him — favors. Sexual favors. It's not been bad, so far. I'm learning, and we enjoy — I'm sorry."

She tears her hand from his and covers her face.

"I don't love him, Cleophas," she says tearfully, "I love you. I had to tell you because it was just starting to feel so wrong, so awfully, terribly wrong. I want to share everything with you. I don't want us to be separate in any way, and it was just starting to feel so wrong. I was keeping something from you and it was terrible and I didn't know how you would react, but I just had to tell you —"

Slowly, Cleophas peels her hands away from her teary face

and kisses her. He kisses her as though she is cracked china, and his kiss will mend her. He kisses her as though she is a rosebud covered in frost and his kiss will melt the cold and open her. He kisses her, unfolding her like paper and ribbons and silk, and she replies like music of strings and pipes and stars.

"Nothing which we are to perceive in this world equals the power of your intense fragility," he says, *"Whose texture compels me with the color of its countries, rendering death and forever with each breathing.* I love you, Blathnat. I will never stop loving you. I've always known what you are like, and I can't change that. Nor do I want to. You're beautiful, Blathnat. I want you to be happy. Continue take your lessons with Roi. You know me more than anyone, just the way I know you. We unclose each other. I love you."

"I love you too," she says, hiccupping, and wraps her arms around him, burrowing her face in his neck. "Thank you," she murmurs.

Cleophas holds her close, breathing in her unique, familiar smell. He doesn't smell the sex on her now, but now that he's aware, he realizes he's smelt it before. He locks his fingers around her back. It doesn't matter to him. He is just glad she has told him, that the burden has been lifted from her shoulders.

"I love you," he whispers again.

The smell of the lily perfume lingers in his nose long after the last floats have passed. Cleophas and Blathnat huddle on the ledge, their coats mingling together. Cleophas rests his head on Blathnat's shoulder.

"Can you hear the stars?" he asks.

She responds after a minute.

"Yes."

"What are they saying?"

"They're singing. But, oh—they're sad. They're terribly sad."

"Why?"

"I don't know why. It's about something that's going to happen, that has happened, they say. Cleophas, they're so sad. They're crying."

"You'll see them one day," he tells her, "Soon. Maybe they'll be able to hear you then."

"I hope so," she says, "I hope so, too."

They fall asleep precariously on the ledge, waking to leave in the morning before the sun begins to show. As they both sit on the hoverbike, Blathnat's arms wrapped around his waist, Cleophas is tempted for once to stay and experience the sunrise. He has seen it in scans and pictures and movies, but never for himself. He wants to feel the gold on his face, the warmth and light. Blathnat snuggles her face into the bowl of his neck, and he turns on the ignition.

Soon.

TWENTY-THREE

Due to the increasing activity of the Xs the date for the move has been changed to July first. There were many who wanted to refute the idea, but fear is a tall tower, and ultimately it won. Now that the barricade has been constructed, more time can be put into securing the items of the Archive, though Dana still spends a lot of time making explosives.

They tuck Kassia in together one night, Quillan and her, talking quietly as they walk back to the Creares'. Passing Snitches stop to say hello to Dana as they walk; she has risen to become quite a figure of importance within the Witch Market over the past month and a half.

Dante is slumped in his armchair when the two of them enter. He is hugging an armful of books to his chest, a bottle of scotch whiskey grasped in one hand.

Dana puts a hand on Quillan's chest.

"I'll handle this," she murmurs.

"I love him, too," Quillan says, pressing a kiss to the side of her head.

Dana waits until Quillan has closed the door behind him to approach her father.

"Hi, Dad," she says, picking her way across the floor. There is grey stubble on Dante's face. She sits on a box across from him.

"You never really realize how much you love something until you're forced to lose it, do you?" he says.

Two of the books begin to slip from his arms and he jumbles them to reclaim them all.

"I mean you can care about them as much as you do, can forge amazing memories with them, but it all surges back to you when you have to leave them," he says.

Dana looks closer at the books and realizes that they are the American editions of all seven *Harry Potter* novels. Dante's eyes are somber as he looks at her.

"I can't leave them, Dana," he says chokingly, "I have so many and I can't take them all, but I can't leave these ones."

As much as Dante loves history, he adores fantasy. His copies of *Harry Potter* are the only ones in the Witch Market. Dana remembers being read to late into the night about the adventures of Harry, Ron, and Hermione; even she has a special fondness for the stories.

"Where did you get this?" she asks, reaching forward and plucking the nearly empty bottle of scotch from his hand.

"Got it from Leon," Dante says.

Dana has never seen her father under this amount of despair before. The sight of him drinking spirits is a beacon; like herself, Dante drinks wine regularly, but he only falls upon the bottle when very stressed.

Dana rarely forges material attachments; she can only imagine what he must be going through. She tries to think of the things she cannot do without; Maria V. Snyder's *Poison Study* books, her electric stick, her explosion kit— but still, she thinks, as much as she values them, she could definitely do without them. Not even Hewett quite qualifies, she thinks, feeling rather guilty. Of course she would probably cry if the owl died; she's not insensitive, but she would move on eventually. Her crutch is probably the only material thing she relies on. Dana is more attached to people than things. Her family, Cleophas, Quillan. They are her strength and sustenance. She can't imagine losing either of the boys.

Dana takes a swig of the scotch and instantly regrets it. She rarely drinks spirits, preferring wine, and the foul-tasting liquid burns her throat on the way down.

"Dad," she says, putting the bottle aside, "We can bring the books. We can. We'll make room."

"It's not just these," Dante says, "It's all of them, all of the great stories—*The Lord of the Rings, A Wrinkle In Time,* and damn him if Darcy doesn't take *The Chronicles of Narnia* with him. Shakespeare and Austen and Bronte and Dickens and

Twain, they're all packed away, everyone loves them, but it's these stories that I care about the most, Dana. The others used to make fun of me, you know. 'Why don't you focus on your history and mythology,' they'd say, 'No one will remember your children's stories'. But they do, Dana, they *do*. I can't count the number of times I've lent these books out to families and lonely people. People love these stories. They may not be mythical, but they have magic of another sort.

"I grew up in the Witch Market, just like you, and when an extermination would happen outside, I would huddle in my bed and read *The Sorcerer's Stone*. Partly it was to pass the time, but it was a great comfort to me too. It still is today. I love these stories, and if I have to carry them on my back to New Hampshire, I will."

Dana lays a hand on his knee.

"We'll find a way," she tells him, "We will."

Dante's dark amber eyes meet her midnight ones. They are low-lidded, always giving him a slightly sleepy look. Tonight they are sunk even lower, and Dana thinks he's probably drunk.

"You are a grand one," he says, "Have you noticed? A grand person, Dana. You've done so much for all of us. I'm honored to have you for a daughter."

"Thank you," Dana says, not knowing what to say. She gets up and plants a kiss on Dante's head.

"Don't stay up too late, Dad."

Solitude heals in the Creare house. Dante will be better in the morning.

* * *

While in bed, Dana catalogues the progress that has been made and what's left that needs to be done. Now there are eight working hovervans, with only one more that needs to be fixed up. The walking and riding parties have been decided upon, after a great deal of heckling. Bit by bit, the vans are filling up with possessions and pieces of the Archive, but Dana can feel the Snitches realizing that not everything will be able to get transported. Now that the barricade in front of the south door is built, people have begun to ask more questions about the Xs. Dana has been revealing the details of the defense plan in pieces; how many electric sticks and crossbows there are, and giving the specifications and velocity of the explosives and grenades she has been making.

Dana sighs and rolls onto her side. Always her left side, ever since the accident years ago. That was the most disappointing day of her life, the worst day. The day she blew half her room away and with it mangled her right leg for life. She will never forget the look on her parents' faces when they told her she would no longer be able to run, not even walk properly any more. It is the most disappointed she has ever felt, the most humiliated. Ever since, she has fought to become the strongest she can be, for herself and everyone around her.

Quillan does not know, but when he told her Klaudia was killed in the extermination, it took something out of her. Dana always favored Klaudia over Kassia; the girl had spirit and vigor. She was a rambunctious thing, a fierce little creature. Klaudia was born with her bad leg, but she never let it deter her. She didn't use a crutch like Dana, hobbling around after Kassia wherever she went, though usually Klaudia was the leader.

Thinking about Klaudia makes her wish Quillan was in her bed. Her room feels lonely, swathed in the slight lantern light that shines through the small circle window. She has not told him she's carrying his child. He'll find out when he needs to, she thinks, but until then, there are more important things to deal with.

Dana's glad he's back. She has always been a protective being, more so over Cleophas than Quillan, and she rarely lets down her guard enough for anyone to see that sometimes she needs protecting too. She knows Quillan wants to protect her. He's a gentle, nurturing person. His care is immense. Dana has always been the strong one, holding her ground and keeping her head high, but maybe, she realizes, maybe she can let others help her as well. She doesn't have to preserve herself on her own. Life may be a journey of self-preservation, but she doesn't have to take it in solitude.

Dana closes her eyes and pulls the blankets tighter around her. She imagines Quillan cuddling her, his body curled around her own, like one fiddlehead. She allows herself to think of New Hampshire; fields and forests, green and verdant and alive.

Alverdine sat her down a few days ago with a botany book. She showed her the state plants of New Hampshire, the purple lilac and the lady's slipper. Dana mulls the plants over, and Quillan comes to mind with the lady's slipper. It is a dainty, delicate flower, tender and sweet, and she is reminded of him. She is much more like the lilac, hardy and strong.

Maybe they can live together after the move. Maybe they can have a garden. Dana will fill it with lilacs and lady's slippers.

TWENTY-FOUR

As he sits on the ground before the barrier that blocks the south door, Cleophas wonders if he will miss the Witch Market. True, he grew up on the tent planes outside, away from the security which the confines of the Witch Market grant, but the Witch Market is just as much his home. Indeed, the whole of BostonMaxia itself is a home of sorts to Cleophas; he has followed its streets and kept its secrets all his life.

There is a morose, dingy sort of beauty to the Witch Market. It is a lopsided place, a fruitful mesh of different cultures and civilizations. Cleophas wonders if he will miss the light of the paper lanterns strung overhead, casting their baubles of color onto the palette of faces below. He hopes they can find a way of reconstructing the lanterns at their new homes. For years, they have reminded him of suns and moons and stars, colorful balls of flame painting warmth and comfort and dreams.

The barricade before him reminds him of that massive

construction in *Les Miserables*, when the poor students of France stacked pianos and tables and chairs to form a feeble, yet defiant boundary against their adversary. This barricade is more technically constructed. Pieces of it can come away without the whole crumbling, to create a gap for the hovervans to fit through when the time comes for them to take the left tunnel out to the freeway.

There is only one week left until the move. All personal possessions and provisions have been bundled together, waiting in packs for when they will be slung over shoulders for the walking party's northern trek. As much of the Archive as possible has been packed away, but there is still much that cannot be saved. Cleophas has witnessed hordes of weeping Snitches pouring in and out of the open doors to say goodbye and to commit to memory the sights and sounds they will be leaving behind.

Once again, Cleophas's coat is crowded with his personal effects. He has begun to itch with a creeping excitement. As the clock ticks closer and closer to the date of their exodus, so it also increases his anticipation.

We'll be free.

Cleophas feels a light touch on his shoulder and cranes around to see Blathnat standing behind him. Her long hair hangs in limp curtains; unhappiness permeates her.

"Hi," Cleophas says, looking up at her.

He takes a hold of her hand, hanging near his head. *What's wrong?*

"Come with me," she says, and he imagines her like a lily, bending over and laden with dew; each droplet an extra pound of sadness on her back.

They sneak out of the Witch Market and wander towards old Boston, to the bank rooftop they frequent so often. In the glow of the transparent alumina, Blathnat begins to cry silently, tears streaming down her cheeks. Cleophas sits close to her; his hands move from grasping her own to wrapping around her thin body. He wants to ask the cause of her wretchedness, but knows she will not answer him. He does not need a reason to comfort Blathnat. He never has. She cries and he holds her, afraid to move his arms in case she crumbles like an old marble statue.

They fall asleep there on the roof, holding onto each other like otters. Cleophas wakes, eyelids fluttering like butterfly wings, to see Blathnat watching him with her gold coin eyes, blue hair turned to a cloud by the light of the transparent alumina. Cleophas's breath catches in his mouth like a moth trapped in a lantern; her beauty is enchanting, and his heart palpitates like wings. Blathnat's long fingers move over his face, touching down like snowflakes, the pads of her fingers brushing over his eyelashes. They trail down his nose, over

247

the curvature of his lips, beneath the layers of his coat and shirt to hum across his collarbone. Blathnat kisses him, her smell washing over him like a wave, and Cleophas quickly links his hand with her free one, desperate for some piece of her to hold tight to. She is a force, he remembers, as with each touch they open wider and wider a rose.

Their clothes are shed like petals, and together they blossom as one flower. Blathnat's kisses travel all over his body, and Cleophas does his best to return them, knowing she is much more experienced at this type of thing, but he soon lets go of that thought as easily as one lets go of a bunch of balloons.

When he trembles, Blathnat kisses him softer, like lush moss beside a river, and daisies painted with sun. She plants roses on his skin with her lips and tongue, rose blossoms that unfold in snow.

Cleophas never once lets go of her hand.

At one point he wraps all of his limbs around her, longing to claim her as she has claimed him, and Blathnat's hair falls over them both as she kisses him. Their bodies are like sand and stardust, their life force contained only by the delicate skin they wear. Cleophas has always been excited by just the slightest touch of their skin, and now he feels as though he could explode into a million pieces and burst into the night like fireflies.

At the end—and how Cleophas wishes it doesn't have to end—they cuddle in a nest of their clothing, blanketed by Blathnat's coat and their own heat. Cleophas feels warm and cozy, snug against her body, and he presses a sticky kiss to Blathnat's cheek. The smell of her is stuck to him, languid and carnal. They look at each other, and Blathnat begins to laugh, a smile appearing on her face. Her eyes crinkle into the stars she talks about so often, and her laughter ignites something in Cleophas, who giggles. His giggles give way to fully-fledged laughs, and soon the two of them are squirming with silly laughter. When eventually the laughter subsides, Blathnat turns onto her side and says, "I love you."

Her voice is warm and full.

Cleophas gives her an Eskimo kiss.

"I love you, too."

Blathnat rolls over, rummaging in her coat for something.

"What are you doing?"

"Hold on."

She sits up with a bracelet cupped in her hands like a baby bird. The bracelet is large and chunky, but graceful in appearance; it is a wolf carved of aquamarine stone. Blathnat takes Cleophas's hand and slides it onto his wrist.

"Keep it," she says.

"Where did you get this?" Cleophas asks, staring at the bracelet in awe.

"It was my mother's," she says, watching him with big eyes.

"Blathnat, I can't keep this —"

"No, please," she says, "I want to give something to you, like you gave me the poem. I want you to always have a piece of me to hold onto."

"You already have," he says, kissing her.

"Keep it," she whispers into his mouth.

On the bank rooftop, Cleophas spells his agreement out over her body.

TWENTY-FIVE

Two days before the move, Dana prays when she wakes. She prays as she has done for the past week now, prays that today will not be the day that the Xs choose to enter the Witch Market; prays that the Snitches will not have to use their cache of weapons; that the barricade before the south door is only a precaution, never to be utilized. Each day, she cannot help but grow more and more anxious; but fear is not the only contributor to her excitement.

Two days.

Dana sinks into her pillow, curling up in the warmth of her bed. Two days and then this will all be behind them. They will have normal lives, peaceful lives, no longer ridden with destruction and grief.

She feels nauseous as she gets up and takes time to steady herself before leaving her room.

Quillan is in the main room eating breakfast with Fontaine and Alverdine. Dana gives him a kiss as she passes, a rare gesture of intimacy. She can taste the toast from his mouth in her own as she rummages in the kitchen.

"How's Dad?" she asks, dropping a teabag in the leftover hot water.

"He's asleep," her mother replies, "Was he drunk last night?"

"Yes," Dana says, "He was upset about the books. I told him we'll bring them."

"We will," Alverdine confirms.

Dana sits down in her father's armchair, tea in hand.

"Where's Kassia?" she asks Quillan.

"With my dad," he says, "I thought it would be good for them to spend more time together."

"How is he?" Alverdine asks.

"Better. It's a slow process, but he's better."

After breakfast, Quillan takes Dana's hand and leads her out of the house and through the Witch Market. He does not answer when she asks where they are going, and Dana soon discovers that they have no set destination as they walk long loops through the Witch Market, frequenting little side streets and winding roads.

"I wonder if anyone will ever find this place after we're gone," Quillan muses aloud, "I wonder, if the Xs get in, if they'll burn it all or if they'll leave it be once they see everyone's gone. Maybe some teenagers from Lower City will be exploring one day and stumble upon it. Wouldn't that be so cool? Wandering along and finding yourself in the remains of this whole secret civilization."

Dana looks at him and sees his eyes are full of awe.

"Of course, all the houses will be empty. It'll be like a ghost town; just an empty shell of what it used to be. Everyone will be gone."

"Do you think they'll ever reverse the Culture Wipe?" he asks a while later.

"No," Dana responds, "I think it's unlikely. You've heard what Cleophas says about the New Culture Celebration- they love it up there. The whole country does."

"Not the whole country," Quillan corrects, "A few states voted against it, remember?"

"Yes. That's why we're going to New Hampshire."

"Maybe it will turn around one day. Maybe we could change things, Dana."

"Let's leave the Witch Market first," she says.

"Are you still going to walk—?"

"Yes, I am."

Ever since they began speaking again, Quillan has been trying to convince Dana to ride in the hovervans, but she is having none of it.

"Kassia's walking and she's nine," she says.

"She's only walking because she's like you," Quillan

grumbles, "She's getting more and more stubborn. It reminds me of Klaudia."

Dana doesn't know what to say to that except to hold his hand. She's never been very good at dealing with other people's grief. Holding Quillan's hand is awkward with her crutch, as it makes her walk even more lopsidedly, and after a while she lets go.

"I love you," she says, when there is no one around but the two of them.

Quillan's hand snakes around her shoulders and he plants a kiss in her curly hair.

"I know you do," he says, "I love you, too."

Dana is glad that there is no one around when he begins kissing her more avidly, all over her face, alighting on her mouth between other visitations to her nose, ears, and cheeks. She doesn't like it when other people have a window into their relationship. It's a private thing, she thinks.

Dana has started returning his kisses and the whole affair is getting a bit too vigorous for public space when she notices Cleophas out of the corner of her eye.

"Cleophas!" she exclaims, pushing Quillan away.

The boy stands there sheepishly, looking amused but also utterly bashful and ashamed. Seventeen years old, but he is such a child.

"Hi," he mumbles.

Quillan starts laughing, and Cleophas cracks a coy smile.

"Oh, shut up," Dana says, thumping Quillan's chest.

Together, the three of them walk around the Witch Market, taking in the changed sights. Snitches pass in groups, helping each other empty their houses and pack their possessions into bags for the walking party. Others continue to stuff the contents of the Archive into the hovervans, taking up as much space as possible while still leaving room for the additional passengers. Walking through the hothouse, they see that even that has been emptied, as the smaller plants and seeds are fitted into the vans. Only half-full beds of herbs and vegetables and the fruit trees remain. They sit under a few slim cherry trees and pick the last fruits from its dainty branches.

"Do you think you'll miss it?" Cleophas asks as they recline.

"Miss what?"

"This place."

"No," Dana says.

"I think I'll miss some of it," Quillan says, plucking a pit from his mouth and tossing it across the hothouse. "Just what I've become accustomed to over the years; the sounds, the smells. But I'm looking forward to a proper house eventually. Maybe we'll even get jobs."

"What kind of job would you have?" Dana asks. She thinks the notion somewhat incredulous.

"I want to be a librarian, or a historian," he says.

"You wouldn't get any funding for it though."

"Of course I would. It could be a library just for the Snitches. People could volunteer there; our community could fund it. I don't think it would take a lot of money to run a library. And we have all of its contents already."

"You could do it," Cleophas says.

Dana waits for him to say more, but he leaves it at that. She will never cease to be amazed by his easy faith.

"What do you want to do, Dana?" Quillan asks.

"I don't know," she says, "I've never thought about it before. I can't really afford to think about it yet; I'm too preoccupied with the move."

"But we'll be out of here soon," Quillan says with a grin.

"You'd be a good mechanic," Cleophas says thoughtfully, "People always need someone to fix things, and you're good with machines and tools."

Dana has always thought of herself as a destroyer, never a creator, but Cleophas makes a good point. Maybe she could fix things. She's better with machines and chemicals than people anyways. People are volatile; they have no rules.

The hours go by as they talk, their voices filling the space of the hothouse. Dana can't remember the last time the three of them have had time to themselves; it must have been before the extermination. Quillan coaxes Cleophas to tell them more about the New Culture Celebration, and Quillan plays with his telekinesis. Dana watches contentedly as he makes leaves and small stones float around them.

It is the first time in a long time that Dana has been able to quell her anxiety. She does not think of her pregnancy, of the move, of the Xs. Beneath the cherry trees with Quillan and Cleophas, she feels at peace.

TWENTY-SIX

When Dana and Quillan head to the Archive to help with the end of packing, Cleophas goes back to the Ektoses house. He told Gamma and Grand he would have lunch with them. They've adjusted well to the preparations and the packing, and Cleophas has helped them strip the Ektos house down to the bare minimum. Even his father has helped some, though Cleon spends most of his time supervising the heavy lifting from the Archive to the hovervans. The move has brought excitement back to him, though he is still curt and reserved towards Cleophas.

Cleophas's mind wanders to Helminette as he walks. Gamma talks about her enthusiastically and often, wondering how she is coping with Redman and wishing they were able to communicate. Cleophas will be glad to see her again, once the move is finished. Maybe they can reconnect then and try their best to continue being the family they were before Brigitte's death.

Cleophas is rounding the corner onto his street when

Blathnat hurdles towards him in a rush of pink and blue. He catches her in his arms and is shocked to feel her trembling violently. Her sobs make her words almost incomprehensible as he tries to get her to relay what happened.

Together they sink onto the side of the road and Cleophas makes gentle cooing noises as Blathnat cries. He rubs his arms up and down her back, terrified and shaken by her distress.

"What happened?" he asks softly, "What happened?"

"It's Roi," she says, "Roi, my tutor. He's been terrible to me. He doesn't teach me, not really—all we do is have sex and I hate it—he was never interested in teaching me English, all he wanted was me. I went to see him after the other night, because I wanted to end it, and he wouldn't let me—he kept threatening me and—"

"Did he rape you?" Cleophas asks, horrified.

Blathnat shudders.

"No. He tried to touch me and I slapped him, and then I left before he could do anything else."

"Then you don't have to ever go back, not ever."

"But Cleophas, he told me he would tell the Xs if I didn't come back, he said he would tell them about the Witch Market."

"He knows about the Witch Market?"

"He learned about it through me, I'm sorry. I didn't tell him much— most of it he guessed at over time and I only confirmed it, you know how I talk a lot. He's smarter than the rest of them, Cleophas, and I don't want him to do anything, not with the move so close. I'm so worried of what he'll do if I don't go back to him, and I don't know how long he'll wait, but I'm so scared of what he'll do to me, Cleophas, I hate him."

"The move's in two days, Blathnat, we can get through this," Cleophas says. His heart is pounding. "Come on, let's go inside."

He walks her into the Ektoses' house, treating her as gently as a china doll. Gamma Lucinda lays her down on the futon. She stands to the side, fussing in a silent way as she twists her hands to and fro. Cleophas pulls a chair close, there not being enough room for both of them on the futon. He caresses Blathnat's head, talking in a soothing way.

"Try to go to sleep," he tells her, "We'll figure something out."

Hours later, with evening setting in and Blathnat curled up on the futon, Lucinda brings Cleophas a cup of chamomile.

"You should try to get some sleep, dear," she says, running a hand through his hair. "Tomorrow's the last day before the move."

Cleophas drinks the tea slowly, watching Blathnat sleep and fiddling with the bracelet she gave him. Her breathing has evened out, and she looks peaceful and tired and younger than her years. Cleophas feels an overwhelming urge to protect her, and he falls asleep in the chair at her side.

Blathnat always wakes before him, and as Cleophas opens his eyes to see her stirring, he wishes he could have the pleasure of watching her emerge from sleep himself. Someday, he thinks.

"Hello," he says.

"Hi."

Her voice is thick and soft and a little bit husky with sleep and congestion.

"How are you?"

"Better," she says, and Cleophas wants to wrap himself up in the word as though it were Blathnat's coat.

"I want to go back."

"Why?" he exclaims, all the warmth he felt a moment ago immediately fleeing his body. "What for?"

"I need to do it for myself, Cleophas," she says, "You don't have to understand."

"But I *want* to," he tells her, leaning forward, "I want to understand, please, Blathnat, why do you want to go back?"

"I have to stand up for myself," she says, "Roi brought me down and I want to feel strong again. We're leaving tomorrow; I can go tonight and by the time I'm back, we'll be going."

She reaches out for his hand and runs her fingers through his, looking at him with her big golden eyes.

"I have to do it, Cleophas," she says, "I have to let him know that he didn't win."

"I'm coming with you."

"He would hurt you, Cleophas—"

"I'm coming with you. I can stay out of sight, but I want to be there. I want to make sure he doesn't hurt *you*."

She squeezes his hand.

"Thank you."

They leave when night begins to fall, taking Cleophas's hoverbike to Upper City. Despite their destination, Cleophas feels relaxed as they ride through old Boston and Lower City, Blathnat's arms secure around his waist. He can almost pretend this is just another ride.

As they near Upper City and the great surges of air traffic, Cleophas's pulse accelerates and he diverts all of his attention to navigating safe ways through the vehicles. Beneath the blaring noise of the traffic, Blathnat gives him directions to Roi's apartment. It's in a high-end part of the city, and the towers sparkle with lights like honeycombs and icicles. In the distance Cleophas can see the Cassiopeia, lit up against the dark ceiling of smog.

Cleophas parks the hoverbike in a glass garden outside the building. Roi's apartment is across a short viaduct. For a moment, Cleophas's breath is taken by the sight of the garden. Trees, flowers, and shrubberies entirely constructed of blown glass surround them. They glimmer in the lights of the city like hundreds of jewels.

"See that glass wall there?" Blathnat says, pointing, "You can watch me through there. I'll stay in view. I want you to stay here."

"But—"

Blathnat puts a finger to his lips and her eyes swallow him.

"I won't be ten minutes. The viaduct is short; you'll be able to reach me if I need you. I'll leave the door open. Please, Cleophas."

He nods.

Blathnat takes off her coat.

"Hold onto it for me," she says, handing it to him. "I don't want him to tear it if he tries to grab me."

Cleophas tries to plead again, but she shushes him once more.

"I'll be all right," she says, pulling him into an embrace. "I'll be right back."

Cleophas watches her run down the viaduct and pull a card from her pocket which she slides through a slot in the door. She enters, and for a moment Cleophas cannot see her and his hands clench in her pink coat. He leaves the garden, running along the viaduct for a better look into the apartment. His breath leaves him in a great gust as Blathnat comes into view. He can see her mouth moving, and a man appears. Roi has blue hair like Blathnat's, but it is bright and short and spiky. Cleophas watches as they begin to talk, and to his surprise, Roi gestures at her to leave. He moves to show her to the door, but Blathnat backs away out of his reach. Cleophas desperately wishes he could hear like Quillan when the movements of their hands become more animated, growing angry with each other. A woman appears in the doorway Roi came through and Cleophas starts. She looks terribly familiar, with her dark skin and straight red hair parted down the middle, and suddenly Cleophas realizes that she is the woman with the butter-colored eyes whom he saw at the party on the Cassiopeia in May. Though he cannot smell it now, he remembers her perfume.

He watches as the woman with the butter-colored eyes begins to yell, her mouth moving furiously behind the glass wall. She points at Roi and Blathnat and moves toward the latter. Suddenly she pulls Blathnat out onto the balcony, kicking and screaming, and now Cleophas can hear all three of them. As he begins to run further down the viaduct, he freezes, watching with terror as the woman with the butter-colored eyes tries to hurl Blathnat over the balcony railing. In her attempt, Blathnat grips the woman tightly and they both topple over the edge, coming apart from each other in the air.

They fall through the air, the woman with the butter-colored eyes screaming, but Blathnat does not make a sound, and the lights of BostonMaxia shine like stars.

Then she strikes the side of a building and her body goes as limp as a ragdoll's.

Cleophas clutches the railing of the viaduct, his mouth ajar. He does not feel real, and he realizes that he is not breathing. He begins to choke and suck in great gulps of air, making guttering sounds as he fights his way back to the glass garden. His body is shutting down, and as he sinks to the ground, he lets out a gasping wail. The tears come quickly, and Cleophas is on all fours, choking-gasping-sobbing.

Blathnat.
Blathnat.

BLATHNAT

He rocks himself, clutching her pink coat in a bundle, clutching it to his chest and inhaling its smell.

Blathnat. Oh my god, Blathnat.

Sirens begin to wail, echoing his cries. He does not know

how long he has been in the glass garden.

It registers within him that he has to get back to the Witch Market. They will be leaving in a few hours. He has to get back.

All he can think of as he straddles the hoverbike, coat tucked against his chest, is Blathnat.

It's not until he has almost reached the Witch Market that he realizes that he has lost the bracelet she gave him.

TWENTY-SEVEN

Dana puts the final two *Harry Potter* volumes into her backpack and takes Hewett off of his perch, depositing the owl onto her shoulder. Hefting the bag onto her back, she grabs her electric stick and crutch and leaves the house after Dante.

The Xs began a barrage against the south door an hour ago, and the Witch Market has been flung into a panic. Dana and Neckarios have already organized the exit of the hovervans, and the only people left in the Witch Market are the physically apt teenagers and adults that make up the walking party.

Beneath Dana's organized, controlled mind, she cannot help but continue to berate herself.

We should have left earlier, she thinks. *We should have left earlier.*

With the Xs launching their assault against the south door, the Snitches are exiting through the lesser used north door.

Dana winds her way through the Witch Market as quickly as she can, linking up with Quillan along the way. Kassia clings to one of his hands, her other held by Yeva. Her eyes are wide with terror.

There is a conglomeration of people at the north door, full of wild movement and frantic voices.

"What's going on?" Dana asks Godfreya.

"Some people have to stay behind to close the door," she explains.

The arguing escalates louder and louder until Dana grabs a grenade from the pouch around her waist and throws it at an empty house. The resounding explosion causes everyone to look at her, silenced. Hewett flies above her, hooting.

"We need to do this quickly," she says, "Neckarios, how many people do we need to close the door?"

"At least ten," he supplies.

"Fine, ten. Those people who stay behind can try to leave through the other exits- I know there's one near the ventilation grates. Take these as well," she says, unbuckling the pouch from around her waist that holds the grenades, launcher, and other explosives.

No one steps forward to take them, and for a moment Dana is terrified. She does not want to choose.

"I'll stay," Godfreya says, stepping forward.

"Absolutely not," Dana says, "You've got Muga waiting

for you."

"Dana, you can't decide for people," Dante says, "We're running out of time."

"Give that to me," Quillan's Aunt Karin says, emerging from the crowd and snatching the pouch from Dana. "I'll stay here. There's nothing for me in New Hampshire. I may as well die like my sisters."

Slowly, the numbers grow, as long-time stragglers of the Witch Market volunteer to stay behind and close the door. Dana's stomach twists sickeningly as she notices Godfreya crying quietly to herself.

"That's it then," Dana says, as the tenth Snitch crosses over. "We've got enough. I wish you all the best of luck. Thank you."

"Wait!"

A voice calls from within the surge to get out the door. Dana sees her Uncle Darcy emerge from the crowd. He moves to Godfreya and pushes her towards the door.

"Go be with your wife," he says, "Go!"

He takes her place beside Karin at the crank.

"There's not much point in it now," he tells Karin, "But since I'm going to die, I'll die with you at my side."

Karin looks at him for a moment before kissing him furiously.

"Dante, wait!" Darcy says, unstrapping his bag from his

shoulders. "Take these; it's got *Chronicles* inside."

Dante catches the bag with a stunned expression, but he thanks Darcy profusely.

Dana is already through the door, moving out onto the wasted tent planes of old Boston when she is struck by a sudden realization.

"Quillan!" she calls, "Where's Cleophas?"

"I don't know," he says, his eyes growing wide, "I haven't seen him."

And then she hears it.

The noise of the north door beginning to close.

"CLEOPHAS," Dana screams, wheeling back towards the door. She flings her electric stick aside, moving as fast as she can with her crutch.

She fights her way through the last of the Snitches running from the door, and suddenly she feels firm arms closing around her waist.

"Let go of me!" she says as Quillan grabs her, holding her tightly to his chest and pulling her backwards.

"Quillan, *LET GO OF ME!*"

The north door is still closing.

"We have to get him, Quillan, *WE HAVE TO GET HIM,*

QUILLAN, LET GO!"

"I can't," Quillan says, and he is crying, "I can't, Dana, I can't lose both of you. It's too late for him."

"NO IT'S NOT, QUILLAN, YOU FUCK, LET GO, *I HAVE TO GET HIM*, QUILLAN, PLEASE, *I HATE YOU*."

She sags against him as the door closes, its teeth locking into the cold ground. Beating her arms against him, kicking and flailing, she begins to sob.

"I hate you," she says, her voice croaky.

Her mind begins to fog, and somewhere within it, she hears another voice shouting.

"Where's my son? Where's Cleophas? WHERE'S MY SON?"

Cleon Ektos barrels through the Snitches to hammer on the door.

"My son's in there!" he says, thumping his fists on the metal. "Open it up, my SON'S IN THERE!"

The north door does not budge, and Cleon is dragged away by the Snitches.

Dana is still fighting Quillan, both of them crying, when a massive boom shakes old Boston, coming from the Witch Market.

TWENTY-EIGHT

Cleophas runs frantically through the empty Witch Market, Blathnat's pink coat in his arms. The image of the bracelet is on his mind, even as he hears the boom that signifies that the Xs have broken through the south door. He can hear the Xs' stilted marching, and he wonders faintly if the barricade has had any effect on them at all.

He runs to the Ektoses empty, teakettle house, the last place he remembers playing with the bracelet. The house looks lonely at the end of the road, but it still smells like home when Cleophas enters it, despite it being stripped of its décor. The only things that remain are the furniture, and Cleophas finds the bracelet under the futon. It must have fallen off when he fell asleep in the chair the other night.

Cleophas jams the bracelet onto his wrist. Maybe he can still have time to get out through one of his many exits.

When he opens the door, an X is marching down the street.

Cleophas slams the door shut and puts his back against it,

all breath stolen from his body.

He thinks of his family as he sinks to the ground and crawls to the futon where Blathnat slept, wrapping himself in her coat. He thinks of Gamma Lucinda and Grand Nicodemus, riding in the hovervans, of Helminette, safe in New Hampshire, of their father. He thinks of his friends, of Dana and Quillan, and a knot forms in his throat. He wonders if anyone has noticed he is missing, and he thinks of Blathnat.

When he closes his eyes, he sees her falling from the balcony again, and he inhales her smell sharply. He tries to think of her as he knew her when she was alive; bright and vibrant and beautiful, and he remembers their times on the bank rooftop in old Boston, especially the one night when they opened their bodies to each other and he knew her like no one else. He remembers the color of her eyes, gold like coins, the blue dye of her hair, the carroty smell of her feet, and the sound of her voice, soft and worldly and full of love.

The door to the Ektos house opens, and the X marches in. It looks at Cleophas, yellow jumpsuit dark in the gloom and raises its weapon. Cleophas clutches Blathnat's coat tighter to him.

"What's your favorite color," the X says.

As it pushes the button on the underside of its weapon, Cleophas yells, "BLUE."

EPILOGUE

Sunlight streams in through the open kitchen window, pooling in the sink and on the braided rugs. The golden light coats Dana's hands as she washes dishes, fingers thick with suds. She stands straighter, a brace on her right leg. Her hair, grown past her shoulders, is knotted in a messy bun. Stray strands escape to drop in curls around her face.

Quillan stands beside her, drying plates and bowls and cutlery. Occasionally he looks over at his wife, but the looks are not stolen glances any more. He lets the sight of her soak into him, reveling in the sun on her face, catching treasured glimpses of the freckles on her eyelids when she looks down.

Laughter flies in from the garden, muffled by green leaves and the day. As Quillan looks sideways out the screen door, he sees Ray and Cleo dart across the grass, swinging from low-hanging tree branches and emitting shrill bursts of laughter. He watches as Cleo drops from the white-budded limb of a crab apple tree to follow Ray into a tunnel at the base of the lilac bushes. They have a nest in there among the knotted branches and purple flowers, where they spend hours together, snacking on the cookies and lemonade left for them by the fairies they know as parents.

It took Dana five years to forgive Quillan. Five years for her to forgive him for dragging her away from the north door, leaving Cleophas to die in the dark, never seeing the stars or proper sunlight. In that time, Ray was born, and for five years Dana would anger and cry whenever her son asked her about the man that came to the house every so often and spoke in a kind, pleading voice.

For Quillan, his heart had shattered the moment he caught Dana and hauled her away. It broke him to break her, knowing that he was losing not only Cleophas, but all the love he had regained from Dana.

It took five years for Dana to learn to fall in love with Quillan again. During those years, Ray became her sunshine, her rock. Having another human being to care for, so tiny and new, gave life back to Dana. But there were things Dana couldn't tell Ray, emotions she would be cruel to heap upon such a young life, and it was during those five years that Dana grieved for Cleophas more than any other member of the Witch Market, for she had lost a piece of herself when the north door closed.

Five years. They were the hardest years of her life.

When the dishes are done and put away, Quillan carries a tray of juice out to the patio, and the two of them recline on the chaise chairs. The smell of summer is sweet and clean; a breeze rifles through the tops of the pine trees. Quillan closes his eyes, listening to the noise of his children and the sound of the world that surrounds him. The wind brushing through the boughs like multiple dancers; the chickadees and wrens and nuthatches winging through the air and tweeting; the fat, fuzzy bumblebees zooming over the flowers.

Dana and Quillan got married in 2097, the same year Cleo was born. Cleon cried when they told him their daughter's name, and he had to leave the hospital room to compose himself. She is a beautiful child, with Grainne's curly red hair and Dana's midnight's blue eyes. Quillan often has to call her down from the trees surrounding their property; she spends hours in them, talking to the birds that flock in their branches.

Sometimes they talk about how much she reminds them of Cleophas, but not often. They communicate it in the looks they share, and the way they caress her head when they lay her to sleep at night.

"Momma!"

Quillan's eyes open. Cleo is lying belly down on the grass, pointing at them. A toothy baby smile shines across her face.

"What is it, Cleo?" Dana asks.

"There's a hummingbird!" she says, pointing.

Quillan searches the garden until he sees it, the tiny, jewel-like bird hovering around the bee balm. The hummingbird flies over their heads with a loud buzz, and Cleo, laughing, runs off down the yard as Ray emerges from the lilac bushes.

Quillan's fingers trail across the space between the chaise chairs and alight softly on Dana's arm. She wraps his hand up in hers, palming it like an oyster houses a pearl.

"I love you," he says.

"I love you too."

Overhead, the pine trees sway.